'Who the heck

'Well, I know you, ...
her. 'I make it a p...
brides whose weddi...
the mock gravity of...

'And you attend heaps?' Fern snapped.

'You're asking if I'm a professional wedding guest?' That dangerous smile again. 'Hardly that, Dr Rycroft.' He released her shoulders, held out a large hand and enveloped her smaller one in a strong, reassuring grip. 'I'm Quinn Gallagher—the island doctor.'

Marion Lennox has had a variety of careers—medical receptionist, computer programmer and teacher. Married, with two young children, she now lives in rural Victoria, Australia. Her wish for an occupation which would allow her to remain at home with her children and her dog led her to begin writing, and she has now published a number of medical romances.

Recent titles by the same author:

BUSH DOCTOR'S BRIDE
A CHRISTMAS BLESSING
ENCHANTING SURGEON
DANGEROUS PHYSICIAN
DOCTOR'S HONOUR
PRACTICE MAKES MARRIAGE
STORM HAVEN

PRESCRIPTION—
ONE HUSBAND

BY
MARION LENNOX

My heartfelt gratitude to Shirley and Kevin Mitchell, whose dedication
to injured and orphaned Australian wildlife made this book possible.

> **DID YOU PURCHASE THIS BOOK WITHOUT A COVER?**
> If you did, you should be aware it is **stolen property** as it was
> reported *unsold and destroyed* by a retailer. Neither the Author nor
> the publisher has received any payment for this book.

*All the characters in this book have no existence outside the imagination
of the author, and have no relation whatsoever to anyone bearing the
same name or names. They are not even distantly inspired by any
individual known or unknown to the author, and all the incidents are
pure invention.*

*All rights reserved including the right of reproduction in whole or in
part in any form. This edition is published by arrangement with
Harlequin Enterprises II B.V. The text of this publication or any part
thereof may not be reproduced or transmitted in any form or by any
means, electronic or mechanical, including photocopying, recording,
storage in an information retrieval system, or otherwise, without the
written permission of the publisher.*

*This book is sold subject to the condition that it shall not, by way of
trade or otherwise, be lent, resold, hired out or otherwise circulated
without the prior consent of the publisher in any form of binding or
cover other than that in which it is published and without a similar
condition including this condition being imposed on the subsequent
purchaser.*

*MILLS & BOON, the Rose Device and
LOVE ON CALL are trademarks of the publisher.
Harlequin Mills & Boon Limited,
Eton House, 18-24 Paradise Road, Richmond, Surrey TW9 1SR*

© Marion Lennox 1996

ISBN 0 263 79763 5

*Set in Times 10 on 10$^{1}/_{2}$ pt. by
Rowland Phototypesetting Limited
Bury St Edmunds, Suffolk*

*03-9608-49999
Made and printed in Great Britain*

CHAPTER ONE

A BRIDE's thoughts on her wedding day...

That she looked perfectly ridiculous!

Dr Fern Rycroft smoothed her cloud of white satin and took three deep breaths. Uncle Al was waiting. Sam was waiting. Indeed, it seemed that the whole island was waiting for Fern to do the right thing.

The sensible thing. Marry Sam Hubert...

Well, if only they'd be content with this, Fern thought wryly. Fat chance! There were two things that Fern should do to prove herself worthy of the islanders' regard. One was to marry Sam. The other was to come home to stay.

She and Sam both.

Well, they'd be waiting a long time! Fern's green eyes grew bleak behind the veil. Live on Barega again? Never!

'Ready, Fern?'

Uncle Al was fidgeting by his niece's side, worry etched on his kindly face.

Fern could guess what he was thinking. Fern Rycroft might be twenty-eight and a trained doctor of medicine but, with her huge green eyes, close-cropped, flame-coloured curls and smattering of freckles, she looked very much the same as the tear-stained orphan that Uncle Al had carried home thirteen years ago. Her uncle worried about her as if she was still a child.

But Fern couldn't guess her uncle's deeper worry. Albert Rycroft dredged up a reassuring smile for the lovely girl by his side but he saw the same desolation in Fern that had been with his niece through all the years since her family were killed. The same sense of helplessness behind the laughter and the same belief that life was not to be trusted...

Fern's infectious chuckle, her cheerfulness and bright smile had endeared her to the islanders from the moment Albert Rycroft had brought his niece home. 'Our Tonic', the islanders called her, and when Fern had announced her intention of studying medicine they'd joked,

'Well, you won't need medicine with your smile, dear. You're a tonic all by yourself.'

Only Uncle Al saw the misery behind the laughter—the distrust of a world that had snatched her family in one awful night.

'Uncle Al...'

'Now, there's no need for talking, Fern,' the elderly farmer said hastily. Even at this late stage he wouldn't be surprised to see his niece turn and run. 'They're all here. You can't disappoint them now, love.'

Fern looked up at his worried expression and her impish face broke into a smile. 'Oh, Uncle...' She hugged him hard, crushing her gown in the process. 'As if I would. Sam and I have made the right decision.'

'Of course you have,' he told her roundly. 'And all that nonsense between Sam and Lizzy Hurst was long ago.'

'Lizzy's part of the island,' Fern agreed, taking her uncle's big hand in hers. 'And Sam and I are no longer islanders. We'll be back for visits—but we've moved on.' She tucked her arm through his and looked firmly ahead. 'Now, are you taking me in to marry Sam, or will you have a spinster niece on your hands for the rest of your days?'

Albert chuckled and squeezed her hand. 'Your aunt and I would have no objection. We've loved having you, Fern—you know that. But you're right. It's time for you to marry.'

Time for Fern to be safe...

In the choir-stalls, the trumpeter had been waiting for the signal. The tiny church was crowded and there were people out on the headland craning to see. The farming community was stricken by drought and this was a glorious opportunity to thrust worry aside. Faces turned eagerly toward Fern as the magnificent 'Trumpet Voluntary' sounded forth.

The bride stood for one long moment at the church door, looking down the aisle at her future.

Then, finally, Fern let her train fall behind her and started forward.

'What a lovely, lovely bride,' the islanders whispered to each other, escaping from harsh reality into misty romance, but they were seeing Aunt Maudie's gorgeously worked dress and veil and they were seeing Fern's tremulous smile behind her veil.

They weren't seeing the real Fern.

The real Fern was somewhere else.

Fern certainly wasn't this vision in white. Someone else was keeping careful step with her uncle and smiling at wedding guests to either side.

The real Fern was numb.

When medical texts had been too heavy to handle Fern had read her share of romantic novels. She knew a bride should glide down the aisle in a haze of emotion. She should see her beloved turn toward her from the altar and she should catch her breath at the sheer sight of him. . .

How could Fern catch her breath when it was just Sam—the boy she'd known for ever? When it was just the sensible thing to do to marry Sam. The right thing. . .

Well, she should at least look at him.

Fern forced herself to look toward the altar. At the end of the aisle Sam was definitely turned towards her—and his eyes were almost as anxious as Uncle Al's.

That was odd. . .

Sam was the sure one. It was Sam who had badgered Fern for years to take this step. What was he doing being anxious now?

Weddings did funny things to people, Fern guessed.

She made a huge effort and gave him a wide, reassuring smile.

Uncle Al had been directed by his wife to walk *slowly* and he was doing just that. It was taking an age to get to the altar. Time seemed to stand still.

Maybe Lizzy was here... That might unsettle Sam. Fern turned to search the crowd—and caught the eyes of a man standing almost right beside her...

Who on earth...?

This was a man Fern had never seen before. Immaculately dressed in a deep black dinner suit, the stranger stood out from the similarly dressed wedding guests as a man apart.

Why?

There was nothing so different about him, Fern thought, but her eyes were still caught. There was nothing extraordinary. Was there?

He was not overly tall—maybe five feet ten or so—with a strongly built body and broad, muscular shoulders.

Most of the islanders were fishermen or farmers so there was nothing unusual in a good physique.

The man's thick, gold hair, crinkled and in need of a cut, was bleached blond with weather and sun and his skin was burnt brown—but most islanders were similar so there was nothing remarkable in that, either.

But Fern knew every man on this island and she didn't know this one.

The man was in his early thirties, she guessed, mentally flicking through the wedding guest list in her head and ticking people off.

How romantic! She should be thinking of Sam.

So why was she still staring at the stranger?

It was his eyes...

The stranger's eyes were the most direct, mocking eyes she had ever seen. They met hers and somehow locked her to him and it was as if there was some magnetic force holding her in thrall. The stranger's taunting eyes challenged her with mocking laughter—

as if he knew that the real Fern wasn't some vision in white satin but really a child dressed up in play clothes, playing a part.

He could see who she really was...

For heaven's sake... Even if Fern was playing a part, she'd better get on with it.

With a small, indignant gasp, Fern tugged Uncle Al forward, sweeping past the unknown guest and turning her eyes from his disconcerting gaze.

She had things to do.

She had Sam to marry...

Sam...

There was something wrong. Sam's look of anxiety had deepened.

Fern's waiting bridegroom looked agonised!

Sam...

Fern stopped about four feet from her future husband, her face puckering into concern under her misty veil. 'Sam, what's wrong?' she whispered.

'Fern... Fern, I'm sorry...'

The thickset Sam was sweating and pale. His broad face had a sickly green tinge and his dinner suit looked as if it was too tight and too hot for him. Rivulets of sweat were running down from his receding hairline.

Behind him, the vicar looked on with astonished concern.

'Sam, what is it?' Fern whispered.

The trumpet sang out unconcernedly behind them but now Fern's attention was fairly fixed on her fiancé.

'I can't...'

It was too much.

Sam cast his bride an agonised glance, clutched his stomach and bolted...

Fern was left standing alone at the altar.

It wasn't just Sam.

Fern stood in the centre of the aisle, still holding her uncle's arm, and around her the church erupted into action. It was as if Sam's departure had opened a release valve.

There were people pushing past with the same agonised expression that Fern had seen on Sam's face, hands to mouth or stomach...

The church was emptying as if it was burning.

Fern stared around her, dumbfounded.

The vicar was backing into the vestry.

Someone was sobbing at the end of one of the pews.

The strident trumpet died away. The trumpet player let his instrument fall. The trumpeter stared down at Fern from his place in the choir-stalls for a long moment before, with a small groan, he too disappeared from view.

And then, as Fern gazed around the chaotic church, she saw a girl move quietly from the back pew. She was a slip of a girl—Fern's age or a little younger—dressed demurely in black with her mass of unmanageable hair tied back severely into a knot.

Lizzy Hurst...

Lizzy was slipping away, as unobtrusively as she could, and there was no agony on Lizzy Hurst's face.

On her lips was a smirk of malicious triumph.

It had to be food poisoning...

Fern's mind worked fast as she gazed round at the confused scene. There was no explaining what was happening except the theory of a massive dose of something bad to eat.

Fern's aunt was in trouble. Uncle Al turned as Aunt Maud walked unsteadily forward from the front pew and clutched her husband's arm.

'Take...take me home, Al,' Maudie whispered. 'F-fast! Oh, Fern, I'm sorry but I think I'm going to be sick...'

She turned and ran.

Fern's uncle looked helplessly at Fern. 'What...?'

'Uncle, I think the wedding's off,' Fern said unsteadily. 'Auntie Maud needs you.'

Al closed his eyes in disbelief and then nodded. He

followed his wife, leaving Fern at the altar. Alone.

Good grief!

Well, she couldn't stay here. Fern walked slowly to the main entrance, her fabulous bridal train sweeping unnoticed behind her.

Outside there were people climbing into cars and departing at speed. There were also people who weren't even trying to make it home. From where she stood, Fern could see Sam's broad back in the bushes at the side of the church. His shoulders were heaving as his stomach rid itself of whatever was troubling it.

Fern's heart wrenched in pity. Poor Sam. He'd planned this magnificent wedding for years—and now this!

What on earth had he eaten? What on earth had they all eaten?

She started down the steps towards Sam but then paused.

'Some wedding!'

The voice behind her made Fern jump.

The voice was deep, resonant and, astonishingly, laced with laughter. Fern didn't have to turn around to know who the voice belonged to. The unknown wedding guest!

'What on earth have you been feeding your guests?' the stranger demanded. Then, as Fern stayed silent—staring out at Sam and the surrounding chaos—he placed a cool hand on the bare skin exposed by the dropped shoulders of Fern's gown and twisted her round to face him.

'Well, Dr Rycroft?' he asked. The stranger met her stunned gaze with a quizzical arch of mobile brows. His penetrating eyes demanded a response.

'I didn't...I haven't...' Through the mist of her veil Fern met the man's satirical look with bewilderment. 'Dear heaven... This is awful!' Her voice broke on a confused whisper.

'I've been to a few weddings but none as different as this,' the man told her. Incredibly, those eyes were still filled with lurking laughter. 'It is awful, isn't it? You should have made it "bring your own basin"!'

Fern gasped. 'Look, I don't know who on earth you are but this is hardly a laughing matter!'

'No.' The smile finally faded from the dark eyes as the stranger surveyed the scene before them.

It was truly awful. The people unaffected were fully occupied with those who were. There were huddled groups of misery everywhere.

'I guess we shouldn't laugh until we know what's happened,' the man said slowly. He took Fern's hand in a swift, decisive tug and pulled her forward from the church door. 'So, Dr Rycroft...'

'Look, I don't know you,' Fern managed, digging her satin shoes into the ground and resisting his pull. 'Who the heck are you?'

He grinned, laughter returning with a smile that lightened and warmed and made Fern want to smile right back—no matter how ridiculous a smile would be in the circumstances. Those deep eyes dared her to smile. It was all Fern could do to keep her lips from twitching.

'Well, I know you, Dr Rycroft,' the stranger told her. 'I make it a point to know the names of all brides whose weddings I attend.' His smile belied the mock gravity of his words.

'And you attend heaps?' Fern snapped. She shook her head as if trying to rid herself of a bad dream. She was so confused that she was dizzy.

'You're asking if I'm a professional wedding guest?' That dangerous smile again. 'Hardly that, Dr Rycroft.' He released her shoulders, held out a large hand and enveloped her smaller one in a strong, reassuring grip. 'I'm Quinn Gallagher—the island doctor.'

Quinn Gallagher...

Dizziness receded.

Fern nodded. At least one piece of the puzzle was falling into place. She'd forgotten this man's arrival.

Quinn Gallagher was an island blessing.

Barega Island had always needed a doctor but none

had been tempted to a place that was cut off from the mainland by two hundred miles of sea and restricted to a population of a few hundred plus occasional tourists. Barega might be an island paradise but it was hardly a lucrative medical practice.

When Fern had announced that she intended studying medicine the islanders were delighted. At last they'd have a doctor. A lawyer, too, if Sam Hubert came back.

Unfortunately neither Fern nor Sam had any such intention.

And Fern had been made to feel so guilty!

'After all we've done for you,' the islanders had told Fern reproachfully. 'We've accepted you as one of us—it's the least you can do to come back here and practise.'

She couldn't. It would kill her.

So when Aunt Maud had written and announced that the island had a new doctor Fern had been delighted.

'Dr Gallagher's such a nice man,' Maudie had written. 'So responsible and caring. He's a real family doctor. Fern, I know you won't mind us inviting him to your wedding.'

Of course she hadn't minded. Fern had been so grateful that she could have kissed the unknown Quinn Gallagher. 'Invite him, by all means,' she'd written back.

A family doctor... Fern had conjured up visions of some elderly, retiring doctor who wanted to mix a little fishing and rural tranquillity with his medicine.

So why had Quinn Gallagher decided to practise medicine on Barega?

That had nothing to do with her, Fern thought hastily. What should be bothering her right now was that almost half her wedding guests seemed to be *in extremis*. Including her fiancé.

'I...I need to go to Sam,' she said unsteadily, lifting her veil back from her face and gathering her train over her arm.

'I don't think your beloved wants you.' Quinn grimaced. He motioned to Sam's heaving back in the distance. 'I think he wants a little privacy at the moment. You might come in useful later but it's too soon for your Sam to need more than someone to hold a basin. And you don't have a basin,' he added helpfully.

'But what. . .?'

What was causing it?

'I have no idea,' Quinn said slowly, reading her thoughts. 'But we should find out. Let's assume we're not dealing with some deadly strain of the dreaded Bridal Fever—or Wedding Day Plague—and take the most obvious plot. We assume these people have eaten something bad. The normal onset of symptoms after bad food is four hours. What were they eating four hours ago? What were half your wedding guests eating four hours ago, Dr Rycroft?'

'L-lunch, I guess. . .' Fern frowned, deep in thought. She and Quinn Gallagher were standing on the top church step, and they were alone. The photographer employed to take pictures of the newly married Fern and Sam was wandering from one group of distressed people to another. The photographer had the look of a man who'd been slapped over the head with a wet fish. He looked how Fern felt.

Uncle Al was hovering anxiously over Aunt Maud by the car. Maudie was bent double.

'Lunch,' Quinn Gallagher repeated slowly. 'You'll have to be more specific than that.' He glanced at his watch. 'It's five o'clock now. Did you have lunch at one?'

'Y-yes.'

'Then that's four hours ago. The right amount of time for the standard reaction to dubious food. Did people eat lunch together?'

Fern made her bewildered mind concentrate. 'I. . . Yes. Aunt Maudie put on lunch. It was supposed to be for a few relatives from the mainland but it turned out huge. Most of the island was there.'

'And what did you have?'

'I. . .' Fern shook her head. 'I can't remember. For heaven's sake, I was so darned nervous I couldn't eat a thing.'

'Lucky you,' Quinn said drily. 'That's why you're not getting rid of it like your Sam. But I'm not asking what *you* had for lunch, Dr Rycroft. I'm asking what these people had. Let's stop playing the nervous bride for a moment, shall we, and start acting like the doctor you're supposed to be.'

The voice was suddenly hard and businesslike—all trace of laughter gone. It was like a douche of cold water and it had its effect.

Fern's mind stopped turning in meaningless circles and concentrated. Absently she pulled the net veil from her head and ran her hand through her close-cropped curls as she thought.

Medicine first. Her training slid back into its rightful niche and took over.

'Sandwiches,' she said firmly. 'My aunt and I and a couple of neighbours made them this morning. And a huge vat of vegetable soup.'

'What was in the sandwiches?'

It was a crazy conversation. To be standing on the step of the church, still dressed in bridal white, with the wrong man standing by her side demanding to know what was in sandwiches! Fern blinked.

'Ordinary. Ham, egg, salad, Vegemite. . . Different fillings.'

'Sounds like gastronomic heaven,' Quinn said drily, the smile lurking once again. 'But hardly dangerous. And the vegetable soup?'

'Aunt and I made it last night. Everything was fresh. It can't have made people ill.'

'Well, something did.' The smile faded and Quinn's eyes snapped into demanding professionalism. 'Come on, lady. You were there and I wasn't. If this isn't food poisoning then we have something potentially more serious on our hands and we may need reinforcements. Can you assure me that was all that was eaten?'

'Yes!' Fern's voice was practically a wail. 'There was nothing. . .'

And then she stopped dead.

Lizzy. . .

Lizzy Hurst arriving just as the soup was being served. Apologising for being late. Kissing Sam's crimson cheek and wishing him all the best. Saying that she hadn't been able to afford a gift but she'd made something special for lunch—just to help in her small way to make Sam's wedding day truly memorable. And carrying in her arms loaded trays of hors d'oeuvres.

Oysters, gathered fresh that morning, Lizzy had said, but to make them special she'd topped them with grilled, melted cheese and slivers of bacon. Hot from Lizzy's oven. They'd been eaten in a flash and Lizzy had smiled sweetly and said, 'See you in church.'

And Lizzy's triumphant smile as she'd slipped out of the church.

'It'll be the oysters,' Fern whispered. 'I'll bet. . .'

'I beg your pardon?'

Fern took a deep breath. She found that she was trembling. Poor Sam. He hadn't wanted to come home for fear of Lizzy's reaction and he'd been almost pathetically grateful when she'd seemed gracious. And now. . .

She glanced over at Sam's still-heaving shoulders. Their wedding was in ruins. Because of one malicious stunt.

'We had oysters as hors d'oeuvres,' Fern said unsteadily. 'I think. . .I guess they'll have been made with oysters that were off. They had garlic and herbs and bacon and cheese grilled on top. That would have disguised the fact that they were bad. A lot of people were commenting that there was so much stuff on them that you could hardly taste the oysters.'

Quinn's brows snapped together. 'Where did they come from?'

'From Lizzy Hurst,' Fern whispered miserably. 'She's. . .she's a local fisherman.'

'But if she's a fisherman she'll know not to serve bad oysters. She'll have known. . .'

'Yes.'

Quinn's face grew more and more incredulous. 'Are you saying this could be deliberate?'

Fern nodded. She felt like weeping. 'I'm almost sure it is.'

'But. . .' Quinn's mind was racing and it showed. 'If it's deliberate. . . If you believe that's possible then how do you know she didn't just add poison? Dr Rycroft, we could have a major emergency here. . .'

'Lizzy's not that stupid—or that bad.' Fern put her hand to her cheeks in a gesture of distress. 'Look, I know this sounds dreadful and I probably can't prove a thing. But Sam—my fiancé—lived next door to Lizzy Hurst all the time he and Lizzy were kids. Lizzy adored him. She always assumed they'd marry.

'Well, at seventeen, Sam decided he wanted to leave the island and be a lawyer. He didn't want Lizzy. Lizzy hit the roof. She did all sorts of crazy things. Every time he's come back she's made his visits miserable— even though he's been gone now for over ten years.'

'So you believe. . .' Quinn Gallagher let out his breath on a long, slow whistle. 'You believe this is a deliberate attempt at sabotage?'

'Lizzy has an oyster lease south of the island. She knows everything there is to know about oysters. She'll know just when they start to turn—and she'll know we won't be able to prove a thing.'

Quinn gazed round.

'The photographer's not ill,' he said. 'Was he. . .?'

'He wasn't at lunch.'

'Your uncle?'

'He hates oysters.'

'And you?'

'I was too nervous to eat anything.'

'OK, it fits,' Quinn said decisively, and Fern had a

sudden image of him in Casualty Department, complete with white coat and stethoscope. She found the image strong, competent and strangely comforting. 'But we need to find Lizzy and confirm it.'

'I guess. . .' Fern looked doubtfully over the scattering groups of guests. They were nearly all gone now—taken to their cars and bolting like rabbits to the privacy of their own homes.

'You know where she lives?'

'Yes.'

'Can we phone her?'

'She doesn't have a phone.' Fern grimaced. 'And if I know Lizzy, she'll be hard to find. But I agree; she has to be found and I guess I know the places to look. OK, I'll go.' She looked ruefully down at her bridal splendour. 'But I'll stop on the way and get something more suitable to wear.'

'What you're wearing is hardly clinical.' The smile surfaced again. 'Though it's white enough.'

'There's no need to laugh.' Fern drew herself up to her full five feet three inches and glared. 'It's not your wedding that's been totally ruined.'

'No.' He smiled down at her, his lips curved in what almost seemed a trace of self-mockery. 'A pity. . .'

'We're wasting time,' Fern snapped. 'Are you coming with me to find Lizzy?'

'No.' Quinn shrugged expressive shoulders. 'There's work that might need doing here.' He looked across to where Sam was still in deep distress, his lean and harshly contoured face growing grim.

'I'll check Sam before I go,' Fern told him. 'I'll take him home to his parents.' She stared around helplessly. 'They seem to have gone already.'

'I'll check Sam,' Quinn said brusquely. 'He's the least of our troubles. It's not the fit young men I'm worried about.' The laughter had completely faded from Quinn Gallagher's voice.

'There are others we need to be worried about. Lizzy Hurst might have thought she was doing nothing but playing a sadistic joke, but there are a couple of your wedding guests whom this could really hurt. Frank Reid's elderly and diabetic. As far as I can see he's gone home alone—and gone in a hurry. I'll go there now.'

Fern drew in her breath. She had forgotten Frank.

Who else? She forced her mind to run through the list of guests. 'There's Pete Harny,' she said finally. 'You've been here for six months, haven't you, so I guess you know he's haemophiliac. He was there at lunchtime and I think he ate the oysters—but his parents will phone if he starts haemorrhaging.'

'His parents will phone if they're capable—if they're not in too much trouble themselves—and I'd rather treat him before he starts haemorrhaging.' Quinn's eyes were suddenly cold as consequences started flooding through both their minds. 'What a foolish girl! What a stupid, stupid thing to do.'

'She's in love,' Fern said bleakly. 'Anything's supposed to be excused if you're in love.'

'Well, you're a bride and I can't see you poisoning people,' Quinn retorted.

'But I'm not in love!'

The words were said before Fern had time to stop them. They hung in the warm evening air, as incongruous as everything else that had happened this day. As incongruous as the white satin...

Quinn Gallagher stared down at her for a very long moment. Fern stared straight back, her huge eyes defiant. They looked a picture, the two of them; the bride in a floating vision of white satin and the muscular man by her side, virile, capable and commanding in the deep black of his tailored dinner suit.

Bride and groom—from a mockery of a wedding!

'Then, would you mind telling me what we're doing here?' Quinn demanded finally. 'If you're not in love what in heaven's name are you doing playing brides and making island girls so jealous they commit criminal injury?'

'I mean...I mean I'm not in love like Lizzy,' Fern stammered. 'I...Sam and I are getting married for sensible reasons—not for stupid, romantic love.'

Silence.

This was crazy.

She was going mad. She'd have to get out of here.

Fern lifted the folds of her white skirts from the ground and cast a doubtful look across at Sam. Sam would just have to cope with Quinn Gallagher's ministrations. She had to find Lizzy.

She had to get away from Quinn Gallagher. He was unsettling her more than anything else was.

'Look, I have to go,' she stammered. Quinn Gallagher was watching her as a bemused hawk would have watched a tiny chicken's futile attempts at escape. 'The sooner I find Lizzy the better.' Fern took two hasty steps down from the church door. 'I'll telephone if I find out anything,' she called as she backed away. 'Where...where can I reach you?'

'Mobile phone.' The hawk, it seemed, was releasing his prey. Quinn lifted the machine from the belt under his jacket and held it up. 'The island telephonist has the number.'

'Can you...? You will check Sam before you go? Please...?'

'I'll check your beloved,' Quinn said grimly. 'Just make it worth my while by finding Lizzy fast.'

Fern nodded, lifting her skirts high and breaking into a run.

Bridal chicken in full flight...

She needed a car.

There was only one car available in front of the church—the big white limousine in which her uncle had been planning to drive the newly married pair to the reception. It stood deserted, beribboned in white satin, white net over the back seat and a set of bride and groom dolls smiling at the world from the back shelf.

The dolls must be the only happy couple on the island!

The keys were in the ignition.

It was all Fern needed.

Ignoring the impulse to pick up the dolls and throw them as far as she could, Fern wedged herself into the driver's seat. The hoops of her bridal gown welled up around the steering column.

Good grief...

Get on with it, Fern...

She started the car and put her satined foot on the accelerator, all the while crazily aware of the dark figure on the church steps, watching...

She could feel Quinn Gallagher's eyes still on her until she rounded the bend and was out of sight of the church.

It was all she could do not to glance back.

It was the end of her wedding.

For good?

That was a crazy notion. They could try again tomorrow, Fern thought, and closed her eyes at the idea of the reorganisation her aunt would insist on.

Aunt Maud wouldn't be well enough tomorrow. Or the next day either, Fern thought savagely. Fern's aunt had seemed weak and out of sorts since Fern had arrived home on the island and Fern had fretted that Maud seemed to be ageing early. Lizzy Hurst should have calculated the effects her horrid oysters would have on people like Aunt Maud.

Quinn would be learning the effects of the poison on the island's invalids right now, Fern thought bleakly, and for a wild moment she wished that she was driving beside him to check on the two islanders they were concerned about.

'I should be wishing I was staying with Sam,' she corrected herself, and knew that she didn't wish it in the least. Sam would be devastated.

She swore at the road in front and shoved her foot

harder on the accelerator. The bridal car sped forward with undignified haste.

What a mess.

How could things possibly get any worse than this?

CHAPTER TWO

SHE shouldn't have asked that question.

Three minutes later Fern pulled up outside the home of her aunt and uncle and raced inside. She had two minutes to climb into some jeans, she told herself, but she got no further than the front door before she knew that the worst was here with a vengeance.

'Fern. . .'

It was her uncle's voice, hoarse with fear, and he was yelling from the upstairs bedroom.

Fern heard the fear.

Uncle Al wasn't a man to express fear lightly.

Fern took the stairs three at a time, her bridal gown hoisted almost to her waist.

Dear God. . . No!

This wasn't food poisoning. Fern's medical training snapped into place as she stared down in horror at her aunt.

Fern's aunt had collapsed. Maudie Rycroft was a limp, prostrate form huddled against the wall of the bedroom, her wonderful, flowery wedding hat tipped crazily down over her face. She wasn't moving.

Fern sank to her knees, satin wedding gown flowing out around her, and searched frantically for a pulse.

Nothing. There was no pulse in Maud's wrist. None in the carotid artery.

'What happened?' Fern was already clearing the airway, sliding her aunt down to lay her flat on the floor and give herself room to work. Maud's crazy hat was tossed aside, unnoticed.

'She was ill,' Fern's uncle stammered. 'Like everyone else, she was sick as a dog. Maud was sick once outside the church and again just now.'

The elderly farmer was literally wringing his hands.

He stared down at his wife and his face was as bloodless as Maud's. 'And she was so upset, Fern,' he whispered. 'Your aunt was sobbing and sobbing, thinking all her plans for a lovely wedding were ruined. And then she came out of the bathroom and said her chest felt tight and there was pain going down her arm and she just... she just fell over...I couldn't even catch her before she fell...'

It had to be a heart attack. Nothing else would fit.

Unless the oysters Lizzy had given them were so poisonous that they had affected the heart. There were poisons that caused paralysis...

Surely not, Fern thought frantically, the nightmare image of the whole island collapsing with heart pain flitting through her head and being thrust away as unthinkable.

'Phone Dr Gallagher,' she snapped back to her uncle. 'Tell him Maud's had a cardiac arrest and I need him here now. Go!'

This was a dreadful way to treat the uncle she loved—to treat any frightened relative for that matter—but there was no time now for reassurance or niceties. Fern's medical equipment was all still in Sydney. She needed Quinn's doctor's bag and she needed it now!

There were some things she could do without equipment. She had to get oxygen to Maud's brain. Fern took her aunt's face between her hands and blew in her first breath.

Then she let Maud's face go, dropped her hands onto her aunt's chest and linked them.

And shoved down hard.

One, two, three...

Cardio-pulmonary massage was almost instinctive in Fern by now. She could do it in her sleep. How many times had she done this in an emergency situation?

But how many times had it worked? What were the statistics? Something horrible... Less than twenty-five per cent of those...

Don't think of that. Don't. It had to work now. It must...

Please, please, please...

This was her beloved Aunt Maud. Maud was only in her sixties. It wasn't her time to die...

Fern shoved down hard, again and again, pausing only to fill her aunt's lungs with air before beginning the relentless rhythm again. In the hall below she could hear her uncle shouting desperately into the phone and then she heard his feet pounding upstairs again.

'He's on his way,' the farmer gasped. Fern didn't stop her rhythm for a moment. Al stared down at his wife and seemed almost to shrink against the wall. 'Oh, God, Fern, is she...?'

Fern didn't answer. She couldn't. Breathe, push... Push... Push...

Come on, Maudie...

They'd done so much for her, Albert and Maudie. What was the use of Fern's medicine if she couldn't save her aunt now?

Breathe, push...

She needed a defibrillator. The cardiac massage wasn't working.

Where was Quinn with the defibrillator? Electric shock was the only way that they could jolt this heart into starting. How far away was he? How long would it take for him to get here?

Quinn Gallagher was the only one who could save Maudie now.

And then Fern heard a car's tyres screeching, a car door slam and someone was shouting below stairs. She closed her eyes and breathed deeply into her aunt's lips—a breath of gratitude. Quinn...

Her uncle dragged himself from his misery against the wall and managed to yell back—and ten seconds later Quinn burst through the door at a run.

He had what she needed. Fern glanced up and saw the defibrillator in his hands. One part of her prayer had been answered...

She went straight back, breathing and pushing. She had eyes only for Maud.

There was no laughter in Quinn Gallagher now. There was no space for anything.

Quinn wasted no words. He left Fern doing what she was doing, instinctively trusting her professionalism, and worked round her, ripping Maud's gay wedding dress apart as if it was tissue and attaching electrodes with the swiftness of an expert.

Her first impression of competence had been absolutely right, Fern thought fleetingly. Quinn Gallagher was attuned to emergency medicine with the skill of years of training behind him. His hands wasted not a second.

Leads attached, Quinn squatted back on his heels and pulled Fern back with him.

'Now.'

He put his hand on the switch and Maud's limp body jerked in spasm. Before she was still Fern was back breathing into her lips. Breathe, pump, one, two, three...

'Again.' Quinn pulled her back.

Breathe...

'Again...'

It wouldn't work.

Please...

Fern breathed deeply once more into her aunt's lips but then Quinn was hauling her back, his strong fingers holding Maud's wrist and the defibrillator put aside.

'We have a pulse,' he said softly. 'Give it a minute, Fern...'

Fern stared wildly down. Her own breath had stopped. She was scared to take the next breath.

'Please...'

She said the word aloud. It echoed round and round the crowded room and suddenly there was an answer to her plea.

Maud took a rasping, ragged breath that was painful to hear but it was the sweetest sound that Fern had ever heard. She stared down as Maud's chest heaved, hardly daring to hope.

Maudie breathed again, and again, and her breathing settled into a harsh but steady rhythm.

'We have life,' Quinn said with quiet satisfaction.

Without pause, he turned to the oxygen cylinder he'd dragged up the stairs with him and started to join a mask to the tubing. The next priority was to get as much oxygen into Maud's starved bloodstream as he could. 'How long without oxygen, Dr Rycroft?'

'How long...?'

Fern bit her lip. There were tears streaming down her face and she wiped them away with a lace-trimmed sleeve. How long? Quinn was asking how long Maud hadn't been breathing.

She didn't know. Her uncle knew...

Strange how hard it was to get her voice to work. She had to...

'Uncle... Uncle, how long was Maud unconscious before I arrived?'

Albert was still staring down with horror at his unconscious wife. He didn't hear her.

Fern stood with difficulty and somewhere beneath her a piece of white satin caught and ripped. Her knees seemed to have turned to water. She crossed to where her uncle stood and gave him a swift hug, then stood back with him at arm's length. She gripped his hands hard. 'Uncle, we have Maud breathing again. It'll take a while, though, before she regains consciousness...'

Depending on how long Maud's brain had been starved of oxygen...

Fern didn't say that. There was no use scaring her uncle even more than he already was.

'How long was she unconscious before I came?' she asked her uncle again, and Albert hauled himself together with a mammoth effort.

'Only...only seconds,' he stammered. 'She was sick and then she slumped to the floor and I thought, what am I going to do, she's dying, and then I heard your car...'

'Then she might have only been ten minutes not breathing,' Fern whispered across to Quinn. 'Maybe even less. And I was breathing for her most of that time. You were so fast...'

'Frank Reid's place is just past here,' Quinn told her. 'I was almost outside the front door when your uncle phoned.'

'Thank God for that.'

The oxygen mask was firmly in place now and Maudie was changing colour. The awful blue-white was fading to pink.

Then Maud's body moved almost imperceptibly once and then again. Finally, the woman's hand moved slowly up to touch the mask and her eyes tried to open.

'It's OK, Auntie.' Fern sank quickly to her knees again, ignoring the ripping sound of satin, and gathered her aunt's hands to her. 'You've had a heart turn but you're OK. Dr Gallagher has an oxygen mask on your face. Don't try to fight it. Just rest and let us do the work.'

Maud Rycroft gave a feeble moan. She fought to free her hand from Fern's grasp and her eyes rolled. Her lips moved as she tried to speak and Quinn lifted the mask a fraction.

'What is it, Mrs Rycroft?' he said gently.

'Fern's wedding...' A tear of weakness and despair rolled down Maud's wrinkled cheek. 'My Fern...'

Quinn replaced the mask and touched Maud's cheek. He was kneeling beside Fern but he didn't look at her. His dark eyes held those of his frightened patient and they exuded reassurance.

'Fern's wedding's a little delayed, Mrs Rycroft,' he told Maud gently. 'We seem to have a widespread case of tummy wobbles on the island. It seems, though...' Laughter surfaced fleetingly as Quinn cast a quick glance at Fern. 'It seems your niece has a while before she passes her "use-by" date. Most brides ache to wear their wedding dress more than once. Your Fern now gets the chance to put her finery on, walk down the aisle and be the centre of attention all over again—without the bother and expense of a divorce in between.'

Maud lay still. She took three rasping breaths, gathering strength. Then, slowly, the sides of her mouth twitched into the semblance of a smile.

'Our Fern always was one for doing things different,' she whispered and closed her eyes. 'Keep her safe for me, Dr Gallagher.'

'I'll do that,' Quinn promised, and the laughter faded.

By the time Fern finally rid herself of her crazy bridal apparel, Uncle Al and Quinn had settled Fern's aunt into the back of Quinn's station wagon. Racing downstairs, sensibly clad in jeans and blouse, Fern discovered her aunt secure in what seemed to be an amazingly equipped vehicle.

'It's as good as an ambulance,' Fern said in astonishment, staring at the mass of equipment inside the vehicle. The island had never had medical gear like this. Maud lay comfortable and safe on a fixed stretcher, oxygen supplied from a tank fixed to the side of the van. There was room for two stretchers but, with only one needed, the other folded away to leave room for Uncle Albert to sit by his wife's side.

'It's better than most ambulances,' Quinn corrected her. He was adjusting a saline drip over Maud. Now he met Fern's bewildered gaze and smiled. 'I'm not prepared to practise medicine by halves, Dr Rycroft, and when I promised to stay long-term the islanders decided to set me up properly.'

'But. . .' Fern's confusion was growing. 'Why did you come here?'

'Why wouldn't I come?' He was intent once again on adjusting his drip.

'No one ever has before.'

'Because it's not a lucrative medical practice?'

Quinn threw her a quizzical look. 'Is that why you won't stay, Dr Rycroft?'

'No. I. . .' She took a deep breath. 'Why I won't stay has nothing to do with you, Dr Gallagher.'

'There is that,' Quinn said drily. He smiled down at Fern's aunt, lying wan on the stretcher. 'But I appeal to you, Mrs Rycroft. Your niece thinks her reasons for leaving the island are none of my business, yet she thinks it's her business to know why I came. Is that fair?'

Maud's eyes twinkled faintly and the sight made Fern feel better.

'Fern was always contrary,' Maud whispered. 'Where. . .where are you taking me?'

'To hospital.'

'Hospital!' Fern stared. 'You don't mean to tell me you've set up a hospital here?'

'Of sorts.' Quinn swung out of the ambulance and stood looking down at her. 'Now, are you happy to leave your aunt in my charge?'

'I. . .' Fern looked dubiously at her aunt. Maud's colour was improving while she watched but the first few hours after cardiac arrest were the most dangerous.

'I won't leave her,' Quinn said softly. His hand came up and he touched Fern's cheek with a gentleness that was at odds with his brusque and competent exterior. 'I promise.'

Fern nodded. She didn't meet his look. She couldn't.

The feel of his finger on the skin of her cheek was doing strange things to her.

Like making her want to weep again.

For heaven's sake. . .Get a hold on yourself, Fern Rycroft. . .

She brushed his fingers away with impatience.

'What do you want me to do, then?' she snapped and then wished she hadn't. She was the medical equal of this man. Why was she looking to him for orders?

Quinn seemed used to issuing them, though. His mind had obviously worked through priorities as he'd helped Fern's aunt and he knew what was needed.

'I want you to take my bag and check on the two patients I was going to see and then come back to the clinic,' he ordered. 'If this vomiting is making people dehydrated then we'll need both of us at a central point.

'I'll ring the local police sergeant and have him find Lizzy Hurst. He can find out what exactly she's done. I want an assurance that the oysters weren't contaminated with anything else. You're a trained doctor, Dr Rycroft, and too valuable now to go traipsing off searching for Lizzy yourself.'

With Albert and Maud within hearing, Quinn didn't add the obvious. Fifteen minutes ago Maud had been clinically dead. She was likely to need all Quinn's attention at any minute and if he was taken up with a cardiac arrest and others were dangerously ill. . .

'I'll be back at the clinic as soon as I can,' Fern promised, taking his proffered bag. She hesitated. 'But don't. . .don't send Sergeant Russell to find Lizzy.'

'Why on earth not?'

'Because I can find her fast,' Fern told him. 'I. . . Lizzy and I are the same age and we were friends as teenagers. I know where she'll go—and if she sees police looking for her. . .'

She bit her lip.

'What's on your mind, Dr Rycroft?'

Quinn wasn't impatient. His eyes were intent, allowing her to think things through as she spoke.

'Lizzy's impetuous—even maybe a little bit crazy,' Fern told him. 'She'll have done this in a fit of fury and then she'll have gone home and thought about it. And she's not stupid. She'll start seeing the consequences almost at once. She's already desperately unhappy and if she sees the police looking for her. . .'

'She could suicide?'

'Yes,' Fern said bluntly. 'I wouldn't be surprised.'

Quinn nodded. He turned to Fern's uncle. 'You know Lizzy Hurst, sir,' he said. 'Do you agree with your niece?'

Albert Rycroft nodded, his hand holding his wife's as if he was afraid to let it go.

'Fern's right,' he said heavily. 'Lizzy Hurst's a bit crazy but she's not a bad kid. If she thinks she's hurt someone as well as lost her Sam...'

'OK.' Quinn unclipped the telephone on his belt and handed it to Fern. 'Take this as well. I'll be by a phone or the car radio from now on so I don't need it, but if I need you I'll be able to contact you. Be fast. Check Frank Reid and Pete Harny first, though, Dr Rycroft. Even if Lizzy Hurst is intent on suicide, she's done this herself and she has to be given a lesser priority. Move, though, Fern. I need you and I need you fast.'

I need you...

It was odd how those words rang through and through Fern's head. They made her work speedily and they made the dreadful chaos of the day become almost bearable.

At the end of the chaos Quinn Gallagher was waiting.

So was Sam!

Poor Sam. Fern thought guiltily of her future husband as she pulled up outside Frank Reid's place. Sam would be mortified that Fern hadn't stayed by his side to hold his basin—but if she'd stayed with Sam, Maud would be dead by now.

Sam would just have to understand. He'd have gone home to his parents and Fern would get to him as soon as possible.

Odd that Sam's need didn't give Fern the same feeling in the back reaches of her heart that Quinn Gallagher's demand for her presence gave her!

Frank Reid's home was another farm half a mile from Fern's uncle's. Fern knocked twice, noting that Frank's car was by the door but that the dogs were still tied. Usually when Frank was home his dogs were by his side. He'd come home in a hurry.

No answer.

Fern pushed the unlocked door inward and walked

inside. Frank must know that she was here. The dogs were raising enough din to waken the dead.

'Frank?'

'I'm in here, girl...' Frank's voice came from down the passage, faint but distinct.

He was in his bedroom, huddled under a mountain of bedclothes. His elderly frame seemed to have shrunk and Fern felt her heart lurch in pity.

And in anger. How dare Lizzy play such a stupid trick. Frank didn't deserve this!

'I thought I'd better check on my favourite wedding guest,' she smiled, swallowing her anger in an effort to reassure the farmer, and crossed to the bed. 'How are you, Frank?'

'I think I've stopped throwing up,' he whispered. 'Though I still feel I'm going to, and my stomach feels as if I've been kicked by a horse.'

'I'm not surprised.' Fern lifted his wrist and was reassured by his pulse rate. Blood pressure a hundred and fifty on eighty. Acceptable...

'When were you last ill?'

'About fifteen minutes ago.'

Fern nodded. 'And you feel like death?'

'St Peter's got his book open, girl,' Frank groaned. 'I can almost read it from here.'

'Well, close your eyes and roll over,' Fern ordered and chuckled as he groaned again. 'You know what I'm going to do, then?'

'Stick something in my backside, at a guess,' he growled. 'It's what you doctors seem to like doing most. I always knew you had a sadistic streak in you, Fern Rycroft.'

'It's a requisite for medical school,' she agreed, filling a syringe from the contents of Quinn's bag. 'I'm just giving you some metoclopramide to stop the nausea.'

'I'm not sure I don't prefer a bit of vomiting.' Frank dug his head into the pillows and swore. 'If I could just see what's written on them danged pages I wouldn't be so worried.'

Fern laughed. She administered the needle with care. 'There. Pinprick, Frank. Admit it?'

'Not on your nelly.' Frank rolled back to look up at her, only the smile behind his eyes admitting that it hadn't hurt too much. 'I don't encourage you lot one bit.'

Fern smiled. She left him for a moment to find a towel, soaked it with warm water and came back to sponge his face and hands.

'Better?'

'Yeah. . .' He gripped her hands suddenly and smiled. 'You're a good kid, Fern. One of the best. It's a darned shame you won't stay. . .'

'Can I do a blood sugar?'

'If you must. . .' He motioned to the bureau, grimacing as another spasm of nausea washed over him. 'My diabetic gear's over there. I knew I ought to do it myself but I couldn't face the thought of getting out of bed.'

'I don't blame you.' Fern crossed over and fetched Frank's kit. Deftly she pricked his finger and produced a droplet of blood, checking it quickly for sugar. What she saw made her wince.

'Frank. . .'

'I know, I know,' he sighed. 'I was bloody stupid—even before the oysters. I had two glasses of beer and a lamington with lunch—things my dratted diet chart tell me to avoid like the plague—so I knew I was playing with fire. And then this. . .'

'Mmm.' Fern looked down at him, considering. He couldn't stay here on his own and Quinn said that he had a hospital. . .

'Don't start looking at me like that, girl,' Frank growled. 'I'm fine.'

'Oh, yeah?' Fern held the monitor out for him to see. 'You need a hospital bed, Frank Reid.'

She expected him to protest. Instead, Frank just sighed and pulled the quilt tighter.

'Yeah, well, I thought you'd say that,' he said weakly. 'And they do look after a man there...'

'You've been there before?' Fern asked in astonishment, and Frank nodded.

'I had a bad hypo and a fall a few weeks ago. Doc Gallagher took me in then—and they made me right proper comfortable, I must say.'

'Them...?'

'Them nurses he employs and that Jess girl, whatever she is. She's not supposed to have anything to do with the hospital but she's a real kind-hearted lady. And Doc Gallagher looked after me a treat.'

'That's great,' Fern smiled. She was a little confused but whoever all these people were it made her job here a lot easier. 'I'll just let Dr Gallagher know what's going on.'

'Bring him in when you come,' Quinn told her when she phoned. 'Is he right to leave alone until you've checked Pete and seen Lizzy? I can send the police or Jessie for him if you like.'

'He's stopped vomiting for the moment,' Fern told him. 'An hour shouldn't do too much harm and I've shifted his phone so it's close to the bed. He's well enough—and sensible enough—to ring if he gets worse.'

Who on earth was Jessie? She didn't know the island had a nurse called Jessie. 'I'll go to Pete Harny's place now and then to Lizzy's,' she told him. 'See you soon.'

'Be fast,' Quinn growled and disconnected.

Fern clipped the phone back to her waistband and turned to find Frank regarding her with perplexity. Clearly the afternoon's events were finally starting to be understood.

'Aren't you supposed to be married, girl?'

'You'll have gathered we didn't quite make it,' Fern said cheerfully. 'Maybe next time.'

'Yeah, well, you're worth waiting for,' Frank said

drily. 'Can't say the same for that groom of yours, though, Fern. Puffed-up bag of wind...'

Puffed up bag of wind...

Fern thought of her fiancé with a slightly guilty start. She should ring Sam's house and find out how he was.

Fern looked ruefully down at the mobile phone as she started the car again.

She was in a hurry. Ringing Sam was wasting time.

Ringing Sam was wasting time...

Pete Harny was fine.

The ten-year-old haemophiliac opened the door when Fern knocked and grinned hugely when he saw who it was.

'Gee, Fern, you look a lot better like this. I like you much better in jeans. You looked a right proper twit in all that frilly white lace!'

'That's what I thought, too,' Fern smiled. 'Pete, you haven't been sick, have you?'

'Nah,' he said scornfully. 'That's cos I didn't eat the oysters.'

Fern nodded. This child was sharp. 'So you worked out what caused it, then?'

'Well, stands to reason.' Pete grinned. 'Mum and Dad were both sick as dogs, though they've stopped being sick now, and the only thing they ate and I didn't were the oysters.'

'Why didn't you eat them?' Fern asked. 'I was sure I saw you taking a couple from the tray.'

'Yeah, well I did,' he said. 'Lizzy Hurst was so insistent—and Mum says when you're a guest you have to eat everything that's offered to you. But I hate oysters—especially ones with gunk cooked on 'em like garlic. So I took some and buried 'em in one of your aunt's pot plants. I guess you'd better dig 'em out when you get home, Fern, or the plant'll cark it when they rot.'

'You have such a delicate way of putting things.'

Fern grinned. 'Are your mum and dad upstairs?'

They were, and their condition reassured Fern. Both were starting to recover. Mrs Harny was well enough to protest against Fern's visit.

'I don't know how you're coping, Fern, dear,' she said sadly. 'What a tragedy. It would have been such a beautiful wedding.'

'It still will be,' Fern sighed, but it was starting to seem so unreal that it was like a bad dream.

How could she go through it again?

Lizzy next.

This was the hardest.

As Fern started the car again, the telephone at her waist shrilled into life.

'Yes...'

'Fern, it's Quinn...'

'Auntie Maud? Has she arrested again?' Fern's breath froze in fear.

'No, she's fine,' Quinn said quickly. 'Hell, Dr Rycroft, I didn't mean to scare you.'

'Why... Then why are you ringing?'

'Where are you?'

'Outside the Harnys'. About to see if I can find Lizzy.'

'Pete?'

'Pete's OK. He didn't eat the oysters,' Fern reassured him. 'His mum and dad did but they've stopped being sick and are recovering. It seems once the oysters are out of the system they're doing no lasting damage. Frank definitely needs observing, though—the vomiting's made his diabetes run out of control and I'm not certain he's stopped vomiting for good. Are you sure you have room for him at this hospital of yours?'

'Four beds, all of them empty at the moment,' Quinn told her. 'Women's and men's ward.'

'Good grief!'

'"Good grief"?' His voice rose in mock query. 'Surprised that someone would put money into making a go of a medical practice in a place like this, Dr Rycroft?'

'Yes,' she said flatly. 'I don't understand why you have.'

'And you suspect my motives?'

'No. I...'

'You're just surprised,' he said.

'No one in their right mind wants to practise on Barega.'

'You mean you don't.'

Fern took a deep breath. 'Was that...was that all you wanted to say to me, Dr Gallagher?'

'No.'

To her fury Fern could hear the inevitable laughter in his voice again. This man thought life was one long joke. He'd found the events of the day one huge piece of comic theatre.

'Well, what?' There was fury in her voice and Quinn heard it.

'I just wanted to say that I wish I could be with you,' Quinn said, and the gentleness of his voice undermined her fury like nothing else could. It drove the air right out of her lungs and left her gasping. 'You shouldn't have to face Lizzy alone.'

'I can cope alone,' Fern managed.

'I know,' Quinn said softly. 'But you shouldn't have to.'

CHAPTER THREE

LIZZY wasn't home.

Fern knocked once on Lizzy's front door but didn't wait for an answer. Lizzy would hardly be here. Not if there was trouble.

She'd be down on the hiding boat—a wreck of an old fishing boat that Lizzy had treated as a refuge since a child.

Below Lizzy's house was an estuary, scattered with oyster leases and overhung at the sides with giant willows. Lizzy's grandfather had planted the willows sixty years before on a cleared estuary bank but the natural rainforest had returned, pushing its way around and through the growing willows in an impermeable mass.

Not quite impermeable... If you knew the way...

Lizzy had shown Fern the way—when life had been bad for Lizzy as a teenager and she'd desperately needed a friend. She'd led Fern down through the rainforest to where the ancient boat still miraculously floated under the willows. Lizzy's family had a proper fishing boat moored at Barega jetty. This boat was one only she and Fern knew of.

'It's my private place,' Lizzy had whispered all those years ago. 'When Dad's giving me a hard time I come here.'

Lizzy's dad had given her a hard time all too often. Her mum had departed, never to be seen again, soon after Lizzy's birth and Lizzy's dad had taken the brunt of his bitterness out on his daughter.

It wasn't all Lizzy's fault that she was half-crazy.

Fern climbed silently down through the undergrowth, knowing that Lizzy was just as likely as not to run if she knew that Fern was coming. Finally, when she reached the boat she swung herself swiftly down, blocking the door to the cabin with her body.

Lizzy was inside.

She was crouched like a half-wild animal. The tailored clothes that Lizzy had worn for the wedding had been replaced by her habitual torn shorts and shirt, and her hair was once again wild, frizzy and free.

She stared up at Fern, half defiant and half scared stiff and Fern's heart went out to her crazy friend.

'Oh, Lizzy, you dope,' she said softly. She stooped forward into the cabin and took Lizzy's hands in hers, drawing the girl close to her.

The half-trace of defiance died. Lizzy deflated like a pricked balloon and burst into tears on Fern's breast.

It was a while before Fern got any sense out of her. Even when she could finally talk, her words were muffled by incoherent sobs.

'Oh, Fern, I'm sorry...I made them all sick and it was only because Sam...I thought...I thought it would serve him right—for taking off and leaving me—and he was going to marry me, Fern, and I love the toad and you shouldn't be marrying him because it's me... it's me... He asked me!'

'He asked you to marry him when he was twelve and you were eleven,' Fern said firmly. 'Lizzy, childhood promises don't count and you know it.'

'Well, they count with me!'

Fern shook her head. She gripped Lizzy's hand hard. 'Lizzy, you know I wouldn't marry Sam if I thought he wanted you.'

'You don't know Sam.'

'No.' Fern sighed. 'Maybe I don't. Not completely. But neither do you, Lizzy. All I know is that Sam and I want the same thing. We want security and we want to be away from the island. And you'll never leave the island, Liz—not even for Sam.'

'I'd be scared to...'

'Well, there you are.' Fern rose, knowing that she was in the best position right now for getting the truth—while she had drawn an admission from Lizzy. 'Liz, what did you do to the oysters to make people sick?'

'Oh. . .' Lizzy hiccuped on a sob and gave a half-shamed grin. 'You guessed it was the oysters?'

'It'd be hard not to,' Fern said with asperity. 'For heaven's sake, Lizzy, you didn't salt them with anything poisonous?'

Lizzy shook her head. 'Of course not. That'd be stupid. I knew bad oysters make you vomit about four hours after you eat them, and I wanted to be sure what damage I did.'

'So?'

Lizzy shrugged. 'So I collected the oysters yesterday and left them out in the sun for a few hours. Then I stuck them in the fridge to make them freezing and get rid of most of the stink. They still smelled a bit off, though, so I added the garlic and bacon. I knew oysters like that wouldn't be bad enough to make anyone desperately sick—I've eaten enough crook oysters in my time to know what the effects are.'

'So you thought you'd just make people vomit and that would be that.'

'And Sam wouldn't get his pretty little wedding and his pretty little bride.' Lizzy sniffed defiantly. 'It's not fair, Fern. Why are you marrying him? You know you don't love him.'

'Sam's my friend, Lizzy,' Fern said gently. 'We both live in the city and we're lonely. It makes sense.' She sighed. 'And your silly behaviour isn't going to alter that. It's just made a lot of people unhappy—and put people at risk for nothing.'

'I didn't put anyone at risk,' Lizzy said sulkily.

'No?' Fern sighed. 'Aunt Maud was so sick and so upset that she's had a massive heart attack. We only just managed to resuscitate her and I don't know what permanent damage might have been done. Frank Reid went home alone with his diabetes and his upset stomach. When I found him his blood sugar was climbing sky-high. I hope there's no long-term damage there but I can't guarantee it.

'I have to go now, Lizzy. Quinn Gallagher and I have our work cut out to try and reverse the damage you've caused. I just hope there's no one we've missed.'

Lizzy stared up at Fern, her face a mask of horror. 'Dear God, Fern...' she whispered. 'I didn't mean... You must know I didn't mean...'

'I know you didn't mean any long-term damage,' Fern said wearily. 'But maybe you didn't think things through as much as you should have. You were angry at Sam and me—but you've hardly hurt us. It's Aunt Maud you've hurt most of all—and she's always been your friend.'

She left soon after.

Fern drove to Quinn Gallagher's hospital with a heavy heart, the sun setting over the island in a huge ball of crimson fire as she did so. Someone should stay with Lizzy, she thought drearily, but she knew that Lizzy would have no one—and Fern herself was too angry to spend more time with her. Besides, Fern was needed elsewhere.

She collected Frank Reid on the way.

Frank settled comfortably in the back seat of the wedding limousine, looking out of place among the ribbons and bridal netting with which Aunt Maud had so proudly decorated the car. The old man was plainly exhausted and Fern kept an anxious eye on him in the rear-view mirror as she drove.

Bother Lizzy.

She glanced down at her watch.

Seven p.m.

The wedding reception should be drawing to a close right now and she and Sam should be boarding a plane to head back to the city. Back to their life away from this island.

She wasn't going through this again, she thought grimly. Not even for her aunt and uncle. She and Sam would have a quiet registry office wedding back in Sydney.

Quinn Gallagher had purchased the biggest house on the island. The place had been built by a movie star as a romantic escape from the eyes of the media. The movie star's escape from the limelight had been all too effective, however, and his bankruptcy had left the vast house on the headland at the north of the island uninhabited and useless.

'The house is a white elephant,' the locals had jeered, boggling at the corridors of guest rooms, ballroom, swimming pool and acres of manicured gardens.

White elephant or not, it was the perfect place for a clinic, Fern thought, as she steered her white limousine in through the gates five minutes after collecting Frank. Quinn Gallagher must have money behind him to be able to afford this place.

'Barega Medical Clinic', the sign on the gate said, lit from underneath by concealed fluorescent lighting, and for an instant Fern felt a fleeting jab of envy. It would be wonderful to be a doctor here. . .

Not here. . . Don't be stupid, Fern. . .

The lights were blazing from the verandah and as the car pulled to a halt Quinn strode from the main entrance to meet them. His dinner suit had been discarded in favour of casual trousers with a clinical white coat thrown on over an open-necked shirt.

The change had done nothing to remove the impression of arrant masculinity about the man.

Oblivious of Fern's reaction, Quinn strode swiftly over and pulled open the back door.

'Did you find the woman?' he flung at Fern as he bent over Frank.

'Lizzy? Y-yes.' What was it about the man that had Fern flustered every time she laid eyes on him?

'And?'

'The oysters must have been left in the sun too long,'

Fern said a trifle unsteadily, aware that if she told the truth Lizzy could be up on a criminal charge.

'I see.' Quinn flashed her a fast, assessing glance and Fern knew that he really did see. 'Then I can assume we should have no major problems.'

'I expect not.'

Quinn nodded but his attention was already shifting fully back to Frank.

'How are you, mate?' he said gently, noting Frank's tight, pinched face. Quinn reached out to feel Frank's pulse. 'I reckon we'll get a stretcher to bring you in to bed, eh?'

'I can walk,' Frank mumbled, but Quinn shook his head.

'Why walk when you can ride?' Quinn grinned at the ribbons on the car. 'Though we might forgo a bit of the bridal splendour from here on.' He motioned to the verandah and Fern saw a waiting trolley at the head of the stairs.

How would they get that up to the entrance. . .?

Then, to her amazement, Fern saw a wide, sloping ramp had been installed beside the granite steps. Chrome handrails bordered both steps and ramp.

No expense had been spared here.

Fern's impressions of expensive renovation deepened the further she went into the clinic. Fern had been in this house once for a lavish party thrown on the movie star's arrival to the island. Then the house had screamed glitz and glamour. Now it spoke of welcoming comfort, backed by clinical cleanliness and state-of-the-act technology.

How could Barega support such a place?

As she and Quinn wheeled Frank's trolley along the main corridor Fern inwardly boggled. This place was worth a fortune and the medical renovations were worth almost as much again.

The room that Quinn steered Frank's trolley into was set up as a two-bed ward, though it was large enough to take six beds if the need arose. It was vast, with huge

French windows looking out over the verandah beyond.

It was a great place to be ill in, Fern thought, knowing that once the sun rose in the morning the patients could see the garden and the distant ocean beyond those windows. This was a far cry from the wards at Fern's teaching hospital in Sydney.

The other bed was already taken.

'Fern!'

Fern's eyes flew to the bed's occupant with shock. Sam...

'Sam, are you OK?' she asked swiftly, concerned. There must be something worse than a gastric upset happening to Sam if Quinn had admitted him.

'Fern, where the hell have you been?' her fiancé croaked from his mound of pillows. 'I've been ringing your uncle's house...everywhere... Finally I had to get Mum and Dad to drive me here!'

Fern gazed down at her intended husband. His normally florid countenance had recovered some of its colour and his bright purple pyjamas increased the impression that he wasn't dangerously ill. Then Fern's gaze moved to Quinn.

Why on earth had Sam been admitted?

'Mr Hubert has vomited three times,' Quinn Gallagher said solemnly, guessing her question. His expressive lips twitched only slightly as he spoke. Laughter, it seemed, was being firmly suppressed. 'Mr Hubert feels there's a very real danger he'll become dehydrated and, after being so ill, the only safe place for him is in hospital.'

'But you're no sicker than anyone else who ate the oysters, Sam,' Fern stammered, and then wished she hadn't as Sam's face tightened in anger.

'How on earth would you know that, Fern?' he snapped. 'You didn't even check. You just went dashing off and you left me...You left me...' The big man's voice rose on an incredulous note of disbelief. It seemed that such treachery could hardly be believed.

Fern winced. She knew that Sam was one who called

a cold the flu and the flu pneumonia but as he was normally an exceedingly robust individual she hadn't been called on for too much sympathy in the past.

Maybe, seeing that he was unused to illness, Sam was justified in being frightened.

She crossed swiftly to his bed and bent to kiss him on the brow. 'I'm sorry, love,' she said gently. 'But Maud was ill.'

'She was hardly as ill as me!'

'Maud had a heart attack, Sam.' Fern was fighting hard to stay calm.

'A heart attack!'

'Yes.'

That silenced Sam for only a second. Then he raised himself on his elbow.

'Your aunt's old, though, Fern,' he said savagely. 'And your uncle was with her. Surely your place is with your husband.'

Count to ten. Count to ten, Fern. . .

Behind her, Fern was aware of Quinn Gallagher watching with malicious enjoyment.

'You're not my husband yet, Sam,' Fern finally managed. She took a deep breath. 'Now, if you'll excuse me, Dr Gallagher and I need to attend to Mr Reid.'

'But I'm going to be sick again,' Sam hissed.

Fern sucked in her breath, fury mounting. How could she possibly have given in to this man's pressure to marry her? Of all the insensitive oafs. . .

She looked down at the bedside table and picked up the shiny aluminium kidney dish.

'Fine,' she snarled. 'Have a basin, Sam. Just do what you have to do and leave us alone.'

He wasn't sick again.

Sam lay back on his pillows and watched with sullen resentment as Fern and Quinn worked on Frank.

'I'd like your assistance, if you don't mind,' Quinn told her. 'Both my nurses are suffering from the effects of your oysters.'

She would have helped without being made to feel

guilty, Fern thought grimly, as she assisted Quinn to move Frank from trolley to bed. While Quinn set up a drip to replace the fluids the old man had lost, Fern gave him a gentle bed bath and helped him change into hospital pyjamas.

It took time to make the frail old man comfortable and by the look on Sam's face it seemed that he was almost jealous. Fern felt herself growing angrier and angrier, especially as Quinn Gallagher made it clear that he was enjoying the whole situation.

'I'll take these blood samples down to the lab,' Quinn told her finally as he filled a small vial with Frank's blood. 'Are you right to finish here?'

'I'm right,' Fern said through gritted teeth. She managed a smile down at Frank. 'As long as you're happy having me treating you rather than Dr Gallagher?'

'You can treat me any time you choose, Fern Rycroft,' the old man smiled back. 'Eh, you're a right ministering angel and that's the truth. One in a million.' He cast a malicious look across at Sam. 'And you and Doc Gallagher work a treat together. A real pair you make—unlike some. . .'

It didn't help Fern's anger—or Quinn Gallagher's irritating sense of humour. Quinn choked on laughter and left, chortling, and Sam choked on fury.

Finally, Frank was settled. Fern checked the drip flow rate, bade Frank a concerned goodnight and Sam a rigid one and walked out to find Dr Gallagher waiting in the corridor.

'What, a ten-second goodbye to your love?' Quinn quizzed her as she closed the door behind her. 'I'd expected a half-hour of passion, at the very least. Don't you realise you can pull the curtains round the bed? Once Mr Reid's asleep it could be almost a honeymoon suite in there.'

Quinn was leaning against the wall of the corridor, stethoscope swinging idly from those long, surgeon's fingers. He was watching the diminutive, red-haired Fern with malicious amusement.

Surgeon's fingers... Fern didn't know he was a surgeon. Why had she thought that?

It was just the man's supreme air of confidence, Fern thought angrily. Confidence? Arrogance. Either way it was something that she usually saw only in doctors who were supremely skilled in their work—and both they and their colleagues knew it.

'Why did you admit Sam?' she demanded angrily. 'You know he doesn't need to be in hospital.'

'I thought you'd like to have him well looked after,' Quinn said blandly and watched her face. He was waiting for a reaction and she knew it.

'And if someone really ill needs the bed?'

'Then I guess it's up to Mr Hubert's future wife to toss him out into the snow.' Quinn grinned. 'Meanwhile he's argued himself in here with all the aplomb of the legal mind. He's quite a lawyer, your intended. I get the feeling your Sam could convince a jury black's white while gargling chilli sauce—or maybe even seventy fathoms under water without air tanks. He's quite a little persuader, your Sam.'

'What...what did he say?' Fern said uneasily.

'Only that if I didn't admit him and he happened to die in the night he'd hold me personally responsible. When I pointed out if he died maybe he wouldn't be in a position to hold anyone responsible, he appointed you surrogate to sue me for the shirt off my back and see my medical degrees torn into little pieces and thrown—preferably with me attached—off the Arnablower Rocks.'

'He didn't really say that?' Fern stared up at Quinn and, despite her anger, she felt the corners of her mouth twitch.

'He did,' Quinn assured her. 'And any man who can tell me all that while still clutching a kidney bowl and occasionally retching, deserves to be admitted—or at least deserves to pay the exorbitant charges I'll no doubt put to his account. Now—would you like to see your aunt, Dr Rycroft?'

Her aunt. . .

Fern's anger faded. 'Yes. . . Oh, yes, please.'

This man had saved her aunt's life. No matter what else he'd done. . .

She managed a smile at this strange, unknown doctor. 'Dr Gallagher, I really am very sorry. . .and very grateful. . .'

'There's no need for that.' Like Fern's anger, Quinn's laughter seemed also to have gone. He stared down at the green-eyed girl before him for a long, long moment and the magnetism Fern had felt in church flooded back in force.

Quinn's eyes widened—as though he felt the force as strongly as Fern but he wasn't sure whether it was a force for good or evil. A force to be reckoned with—somehow.

'I would have done the same for anyone's fiancé,' he said slowly, his eyes still holding hers. 'If he had a law degree and a threatening manner. . .'

'I mean. . .I mean what you've done for my aunt.'

The smile slowly returned, still wary.

'Well, I would have especially done the same for your aunt,' he said softly. 'I'm just grateful we were able to get her back. Your aunt and uncle are two very special people, Dr Rycroft.'

'I. . .I know.'

'So why don't you visit them?'

'I do.' Fern's voice tightened at the old accusations. 'I'm here now.'

'But it's been twelve months since you were here last. You're all they've got, Dr Rycroft. The whole island tells me how wonderful you are but you're intent on putting as much distance between you and the island as possible.'

'That's my business, Dr Gallagher. Not yours.'

'But your aunt's health is my concern,' Quinn said harshly. He dug his hands deep into his pockets and turned to stride down the corridor, leaving Fern to follow as best she might. He kept talking, assuming that she'd scuttle along behind and to her fury Fern found herself doing just that. Scuttling.

'My aunt's health. . .'

'Is suffering because she's missing you.'

'I can't come home just because. . .' Fern walked after the white-coated doctor but his strides were so long that she was forced to a run.

'Just because people need you?' Quinn shrugged. 'Of course you can't. How stupid of me to suggest such a crazy idea. Now let's see how Maud's been getting on without you—again.'

Maud was asleep. Her tiny body seemed immensely vulnerable on the large hospital bed. Fern's aunt was robed in a hospital gown and Fern made a silent vow to go straight home and bring back a pretty nightie. One of her own honeymoon nighties, she decided. In the hospital gown her aunt looked fragile—almost. . .

Almost dead.

Not the Aunt Maud Fern knew and loved. She couldn't die. Not Maud, too. . .

How could she have stayed away for so long? she thought harshly. She should have come back before this.

And by marrying Sam. . . By marrying Sam she'd exposed her aunt to Lizzy's vindictiveness and this dreadful hurt.

There was a pale-faced slip of a girl sitting on a chair beside Aunt Maud—maybe a little younger than Fern, painfully thin with soft, mousy brown hair and brown eyes that were too large for her face. A nurse, Fern thought, but the girl was dressed casually in clean jeans and T-shirt. She rose as Quinn ushered Fern in and smiled at them both.

'She's fine,' the girl said quickly, noting the anxiety in Fern's eyes. 'Her obs are steady and she seems to be sleeping soundly.'

'Thanks, Jess.' Quinn motioned to Fern. 'Jess, this is Maud's niece, the island's wonderful Dr Fern Rycroft we've heard so much about. Fern, this is Jessie. Jess is the island vet but I called her in to help with my humans tonight. She hauls me out of bed often enough to help with her four-legged patients.'

Fern stared. 'I didn't know the island had a vet.'

Like human medicine, animal medicine was underserviced to the point of non-existence on the island.

'I've been here for six months.' Jessie smiled shyly. 'It was a pleasure helping tonight. Your aunt's a lovely lady, Fern. Do you want me to stay, Quinn?'

'I think we'll be right now, thanks, Jess. I'll connect the monitors through to the office and I'll do hourly obs.'

'Fine.' The vet crossed to the door. 'Then, if you'll excuse me. . .I have three babies to feed.'

Three babies. . . Fern shook her head in bewilderment but Jess was already gone.

The island medical service had changed indeed since Fern had last been here. With a qualified vet and doctor it was almost overserviced.

Well, at least the island no longer needed her.

Funny how that thought was starting to give her no pleasure at all.

'Your uncle's gone home to sleep,' Quinn was saying softly. He was watching Fern over the bed dividing them. 'You can, too, if you like. I'll take good care of her, Dr Rycroft.'

Fern swallowed. She was sure that he would. If any man could do it, Quinn Gallagher was the man to keep her aunt alive.

She looked down at the bed again and her heart lurched. Sure, Quinn Gallagher would connect the monitors through to his office and check every so often but. . .

But if her aunt was in a city hospital she'd be in Intensive Care with a nurse awake and watchful at every moment.

After all Maud had done for her, it was the least Fern could do.

'I'll go home and see my uncle and come back,'

she whispered, her voice trembling with emotion. 'The spare bed here is empty. If it's OK with you. . .'

He didn't try to dissuade her.

'That's fine. But I'll keep the monitors going just the same. If you sleep. . .'

'I won't sleep,' Fern said rigidly. 'After the events of today, even if my aunt was fine, I still wouldn't sleep.'

She was right there.

It took Fern less than half an hour to drive home, reassure her worried uncle and be back at Quinn Gallagher's transformed mansion-cum-hospital. Quinn greeted her briefly when she returned but in the next ward Frank Reid had started vomiting again and he had his hands full.

He didn't need her.

'Frank's blood sugars are settling,' he told her. 'Once I can stop the retching he should be OK. I've given him another dose of metoclopramide and it should take effect soon. If you watch your aunt so I don't have to check the monitors. . .'

It had been the right thing to do to return, Fern thought thankfully, as she pushed the room's second bed close to her aunt's and crept under the covers. It was a warm enough night but the events of the day were taking their toll. She felt shivery and in need of the comfort of the blankets.

She didn't undress. It seemed wrong to don nightclothes when she wasn't ill—or even very tired. She was just shaken and she was here to work.

Fern put her hand out from the bedclothes and placed her fingers round her aunt's wrist. This was better than any monitor Quinn Gallagher could devise—and she was a darned sight closer if Maud's breathing faltered.

She was so close. . .

In her long years of training Fern had never felt so close to a patient.

Even with her aunt and uncle, Fern strove for distance. There was no distance here—not now.

Just soul-destroying grief if this heartbeat didn't continue. Maud had to live...

The long hours of the night dragged on.

She should be sleepy, Fern thought, but she wasn't anything of the kind. Her mind was whirling in a million different directions.

Muffled through the heavy walls she could hear intermittent sounds from the men's ward. She heard Frank moan once or twice and grimaced. Let the metoclopramide work, she breathed silently. If Lizzy's stunt caused permanent damage...

Fern was starting to feel horribly responsible herself. By agreeing to marry on the island she'd stirred up a hornet's nest. Frank had to be OK.

Then she heard Sam's voice raised in protest and Fern's grimace deepened. If Sam was making a fuss...

Maybe she should go to him...

Sam had no priority at all.

Fern's fingers tightened on Maud's wrist. Maud's pulse was strong and steady but it didn't make Fern one bit more willing to go to Sam. Her place was here. If Quinn Gallagher was taken up with Frank then he couldn't watch the monitors and Maud had to be monitored by machine or in person.

So Fern lay still, realising that she needed this time alone almost as much as Maud needed her. The darkened hospital was close to silent and the turmoil of the day seemed a bad dream.

The only thing of importance was the beat under Fern's fingers—the steady throb of her aunt's heart.

The monitors were linked to her aunt's breast and they led to another room. Quinn's office... Fern knew he'd still be checking from time to time. A conscientious doctor wouldn't believe Fern's assurance that she'd stay awake.

And Quinn was a conscientious doctor.

The thought was a vague but solid comfort. Maud was safe. With Fern beside her and Quinn in the next room nothing could happen.

Nothing could happen with Quinn Gallagher there.

That was crazy. What a stupid thing to think when she had known the man less than a day. What was it about the man that was so solid...so powerful...?

It was her emotional state, Fern told herself firmly. Nothing more. She'd been emotionally wrought for days in the build-up to the wedding, asking herself over and over whether she was doing the right thing. And, then, as she'd made the decision and the final preparations and made it almost to the altar—to have this happen...

Drat Lizzy, she thought miserably, but in her heart Fern knew her real emotion was one of relief.

'So, maybe it was the wrong decision,' she whispered into the dark, and winced again at the sound of Sam's angry voice from the next room. Her beloved...

He was nothing of the sort!

There were footsteps down the corridor and another voice, softer but firm for all that. Quinn's voice...

Then the footsteps returned, but not as far as they'd come. The steps stopped outside Fern's door. The door opened a crack and then wider, allowing a slit of light to fall over Maud's bed.

Quinn stepped silently into the room. Unlike the corridor where the floor was of polished wooden boards, the wards were carpeted—so Quinn's feet made no sound. His body blocked the slit of light but as he came further into the room the slit widened and Fern could watch him as he approached.

He checked Maud with deft precision. Fern nodded silently to herself. This man didn't leave anything to chance—or to the monitors. He felt Maud's pulse and took her blood pressure, then checked each monitor lead. Then, almost as an afterthought, Quinn turned the pencil light torch he'd been holding to shine down at Fern.

'I'm not asleep,' she whispered. 'I'm not completely untrustworthy.'

He smiled, then, his smile almost tender in the soft light of the torch.

'I never thought you were, Dr Rycroft,' he said gently. 'But your aunt is my patient. Would you like a cup of tea?'

'I'd love one,' Fern smiled. She pushed back the bedcovers and Quinn's eyes widened as he saw her blouse and jeans.

'What, no nightie, Dr Rycroft? Dressed for escape, then, are we?'

'If you like.' Fern's voice tightened.

'I wouldn't worry about indecent advances by the night staff.' Quinn smiled. 'Your beloved's only a scream away. In fact, I would have thought you'd know that. Has he been keeping you awake?'

'He's not my beloved,' Fern said crossly. 'I. . . Is he all right?'

'No.' Quinn shook his head. 'He's not all right. Mr Reid has been ill again and rude enough to disturb Mr Hubert's sleep. Mr Hubert seems to think he'd like a private room—or at least have Mr Reid shifted out into the corridor. Very tetchy he's been when I've suggested he take himself off to his own bed if he didn't like it here.'

'He's. . .he's upset,' Fern said miserably. 'Sam's not always so unreasonable.'

'I'd assumed that,' Quinn nodded. 'If he's half as bad as I think he is then you've been granted a last-minute reprieve from death by boredom. Still, I have to assume you know what you're doing, Dr Rycroft.'

'Good.' Fern gritted her teeth. 'Look, forget the cup of tea. . .' This wasn't a big hospital with kitchen staff on call.

'It's already made,' he smiled. 'If you're as awake as I think you are, come out on the verandah and drink it.'

'But. . .' Fern looked doubtfully down at her sleeping aunt.

'Maud's growing stronger by the minute,' Quinn assured her. 'You must be able to feel it yourself.' He flicked a switch above the bed and a soft, dim light shone across Maud's face. It wasn't enough to disturb Maud's deep sleep but it showed them both her improving colour. 'Now, through those French windows is the verandah and it's a lovely night. I'll bring tea round there and we'll leave the windows open and be able to watch Maud while we drink it.'

'But. . .won't we disturb S. . .Mr Reid?'

'You mean, won't your Sam hear us and demand to know what the heck's going on?' Quinn's teeth flashed with laughter as he shook his head. 'Their window's round the corner and your Sam insisted it be closed because he's allergic to draughts or some such nonsense. Which leaves us alone. An assignation with an engaged woman in the wee small hours. . . What could be better? What a pity I didn't put the champagne on ice. . .'

'But. . .'

'No more buts.' Quinn Gallagher put a finger on her lips and pressed her mouth firmly closed. 'Meet me in five minutes below the window,' he grinned. 'Should I bring my ladder—or will you let down your hair?'

Despite herself, Fern heard herself give a low chuckle in response. This man was ridiculous.

This man was dangerous.

The thought flashed through her mind with the clarity of white light. It almost made her gasp.

'No. I. . .'

It was too late. Quinn was already striding toward the door, his back turned to her.

'Five minutes,' he said over his shoulder as he reached the door. Five minutes to your date with doom. . .

This was ridiculous.

Fern pushed back the bedclothes completely and checked Maud once again. Her check was unnecessary. Quinn's examination two minutes before had been thorough enough.

She didn't want to sit on the verandah and drink tea

with this unknown doctor. Why on earth should she?

Because she badly wanted a drink and she also wanted to stretch her legs. It made sense.

So?

'So have a cup of tea with the man,' she muttered angrily to herself. 'It hardly means anything.'

If it hardly meant anything, why were her knees like jelly?

There was no need for her knees to shake.

The tea on the verandah was innocent in the extreme. Fern and Quinn sat in comfortable cane chairs, a wicker table between them, and sipped tea as if it was mid-afternoon and Fern was paying a social call.

It was ridiculous.

It was also a great way to break the tension.

Over her teacup Fern caught Quinn's eye and her mouth twitched into laughter.

His eyes laughed right back.

'I'm sorry I can't offer you a cucumber sandwich,' he grinned. 'The maid's off duty.'

'It's a lack,' Fern said sadly, 'but I can make do.'

'I thought of wearing a frilly apron and starched cap myself.' Quinn's mournful tone exactly matched hers. 'But try as I might I can't convince myself that frills become me. I make a much better butler. If you'd like to go round to the front door and ring the bell I'll show you my true butling style. Mind, at three in the morning I'll probably ask icily for your calling card and see you off the premises.'

Fern choked.

There was silence again but this time the silence was comfortable. Something was fitting round Fern like a lovely, comforting cloak.

Something that she'd never felt before....

She finished her tea slowly, glancing back into Maud's room every few moments as she sipped. Finally, reluctantly, she finished her cup, placing it back on the wicker table, and rose.

Strangely she was loath to move. This night was her wedding night—and she was on the verandah of another man's house feeling that here was someone who. . .

Stop it, Fern! Stop it!

What was her errant mind thinking? She was crazy!

'Thank you. . . Thank you for the tea,' she said stiffly. 'I should go back in. . .'

And then she stopped as something wet and cold touched her ankle.

Fern stepped back in surprise and looked down.

She was wearing sandals and her ankles were exposed. Nuzzling the bare skin above her feet was a tiny wallaby, only half-grown.

'For heaven's sake. . .'

Fern knelt down. The tiny creature showed not the least fear. He transferred his nose to Fern's hand and nuzzled these strange new smells with equal interest.

'Where did you come from?' Fern asked with delight. She looked up at Quinn. 'Is he a pet?'

'No.' Quinn was smiling down at her, the warmth in his eyes directed at Fern rather than the wallaby. He leaned over and scooped up the little creature. 'This is one of Jessie's babies and he's getting very bold in his old age.'

'Old age!'

'He's been here four months. He's practically a grown-up now.'

Quinn walked over to the edge of the verandah. Hanging from the rail was a wide woollen pouch which looked very like a sweater with the neck and arms sewn up. It was looped over the verandah rail at such a position that the tiny wallaby could jump in or out whenever he chose.

Quinn tucked the little creature inside. The joey squirmed in a wriggling mass of heaving sweater and gangly limbs—and then his eyes peeped out once again.

'It's too early to sleep,' his eyes seemed to be saying. 'If you two are chatting, why can't I?'

Quinn grinned and with two fingers gently pushed the damp little nose down. Like a jack in the box, the nose sprang straight back up.

'He's starting to guess he's a nocturnal animal,' Quinn smiled. 'Someone brought him to Jess after they hit his mum with a car. She's been hand-feeding him—but she's started putting him out here at night so he can get used to a bit of night grazing.'

'Jess. . .' Fern frowned. 'Jess lives here?'

'Sure.' Quinn gestured to the huge house behind them. 'This place is enormous. Jess has taken over the east wing for her animals, and the west wing's for humans. It works well—apart from the odd escape. Even then, the sight of a baby wallaby or an echidna waddling down the corridors only seems to keep my patients stirred.'

'I don't know what the Health Commission would say about that,' Fern said doubtfully, and Quinn grinned again.

'The Health Commission, bless their bureaucratic little hearts, are far, far away and, anyway, if they closed Jess's and my operations down now they'd have a war on their hands. Barega would declare itself a republic and design its own flag on the spot. Jess and I are providing a better medical service to the island than it's had in years.'

'I guess. . .'

Words died away.

The night was warm around them. The huge, golden moon was a glittering jewel hanging low over the ocean, its soft light casting a tunnel of gold across the distant waves.

It was almost as if it was a path, waiting to be trod.

This was a magic night. Her wedding night. . .

Fern gave herself a mental shake. The feeling of warmth creeping over her had nothing to do with the fact that it was her wedding night. She looked up at

Quinn and found him watching her, the wide, generous mouth twisting into a smile that was half-questioning.

'What is it, Fern?' he asked gently, and to her horror she felt the pinprick of tears behind her eyes.

It was just that she was tired. It had to be.

Fern turned deliberately away to look in at Maud. Maud stirred in her sleep and sighed, then settled back into slumber. Maud didn't need her, thank heaven, but Fern wanted to return to her aunt, for all that. She felt as if there was something inside her that was close to breaking and she didn't know what.

'I'll. . .I'll get back to bed,' she whispered.

'You can go to sleep safely now,' Quinn told her. 'I'll watch the monitors but I'm sure she'll be fine.'

'But when will you sleep?'

'I sleep on my feet,' he grinned. 'I'm trained as an emergency medicine specialist and until last year ran Casualty at St Martin's in Maybroe. Part of the training is coping with sleep deprivation. If I saw eight hours sleep in a row I wouldn't know what to do with it.'

'But. . .' Fern stared. 'St Martin's. . . If you were in charge there. . .'

If Quinn was in charge of Casualty at St Martin's then he had to be good. St Martin's was one of the biggest emergency hospitals in Australia, coping not only with local trauma but also the complex trauma from almost everywhere else. A man breaking his spine in the Simpson Desert would probably be transported to St Martin's, and the hospital had a neo-natal team that brought desperately ill babies from all over Australia.

'So what on earth are you doing here?' Fern whispered.

'R and R,' Quinn smiled. 'Change of pace.'

Change of pace! From racing with the best to a comparative crawl! Quinn's income would be a tenth here of the income he was accustomed to—and with his skills. . .

'But. . .your skills are wasted here,' Fern managed.

'No.' He shook his head. 'That's in the eye of the beholder and if I'm the beholder I don't think I am. Someone else stepped into my shoes with enthusiasm as soon as I left St Martin's. Here, though. . . Well, even the locally raised doctor refuses to come home to look after her own people on Barega.'

'That's unfair,' Fern whispered. 'I can't. . .'

'Can't come home?'

'No.'

There was a groan from around the corner of the verandah. Silence as if the groaner was waiting for a reaction and then another groan. Louder.

Sam. . .

Quinn grimaced and motioned to Fern to stay where she was while he went to investigate.

'I should go. . .' she whispered.

'No.' Quinn ran his hair through his brown-gold hair in a gesture of exasperation. 'If you go then your beloved Sam will likely as not berate you—going on past performance—and I don't want raised voices in Frank's room.'

'F-fine.'

Quinn smiled as though he knew exactly what she was thinking. He placed a hand firmly on her shoulder and pressed her back into her chair—and then left.

Fern was alone.

She should make her escape while she could. Fern should walk right back into Maud's ward and close the door behind her.

Fern did no such thing. She couldn't. The night was drifting into something resembling a dream. It had little to do with reality. The moonlight shone on her face and held her in thrall while she waited for Quinn to return.

She didn't have long to wait.

Quinn was back in two minutes, hands dug deep in his pockets and the laughter lines gone from his eyes.

'What. . .what was wrong?' Fern asked.

'Your beloved has a sore stomach.' Quinn grimaced. 'He wants drugs to remove the pain and he grew very hostile when I told him he risked making himself ill again if he had painkillers. My assurance that half the island must have stomach-ache tonight—and they weren't writhing round in hospital beds demanding drugs—went down like a lead balloon.'

'I. . .I can imagine it would,' Fern said faintly.

'What the hell do you see in him?'

'I beg your pardon?'

'You heard me,' Quinn said harshly. 'The man's nothing but a self-opinionated, hypochondriacal bore, and you're planning to marry him?' His voice rose on a note of incredulity.

'That's my business.'

'Oh, sure,' he mocked. 'But I'm asking anyway and if you don't tell me I'll ask louder and louder until that boyfriend of yours yells out that we're disturbing his beauty sleep.'

'That's unfair.'

'You're right.' Quinn's infectious grin flashed out once again. 'But life's like that, Dr Rycroft. Most unfair. Now, are you going to tell me or is my voice going higher. . .?'

'I love Sam. . .'

'Nonsense.'

'I do,' Fern said hotly. 'Look, I don't know what you're on about, but marriage isn't. . .shouldn't be like it is in the movies. Real love isn't like that. I mean, if you fall romantically in love with someone how can you tell who you're ending up with? Sam and I have known each other since we were teenagers. We have the same backgrounds. The same ideals. And when we're in the city we can talk about the island and remember. . .'

'You mean you're marrying the man because you're homesick?' Quinn's mobile brows were disappearing into his hair.

'No. Yes. . . Look, this is ridiculous,' Fern said desperately. 'You have no right to interfere. . .'

'I have a right to stop a tragedy,' Quinn said grimly.

He reached out and took her hands in his, not gently. 'Good grief, woman, you could do better than that noise-box. Do you have any idea just how beautiful you are?'

'No!' Fern's voice was a barrier of pain. She tugged her hands back but they were held in a grip of iron. 'Look, I don't know what on earth you're doing...'

'Well, that makes two of us.' Quinn stared down at her in the golden moonlight and there was a trace of confusion in the grimness around her eyes. 'But I know that there's love and laughter right near the surface behind that practical, sensible mind of yours, Dr Rycroft. And I know one day you'll wake up with that boring little creep in the next ward and think "what have I done?"'

'Why should I?'

'Because he's as passionless as a frog,' Quinn threw back at her, and then that irrepressible laughter surfaced again. He chuckled. 'Mind, there might be some pretty passionate frogs out there, for all I know. If there are, then your Sam doesn't compete.'

'Look, will you let me go?'

'Do you know how passionate your intended is?' Quinn asked. 'You didn't dash to his rescue at first groan. You hardly gave yourself time to kiss him goodnight—and I wouldn't mind betting all he gave you was a peck on the cheek.'

'There's more to life than passion,' Fern retorted.

'"There's more to life than..."' Quinn's repetition of her words died away to silence.

There was a long, long silence.

Quinn didn't release the pressure on Fern's hands for a moment. He stood looking down at her in the moonlight and the expression in his eyes was one of baffled anger.

'If I was your man...' he said at last.

'Well, you're not.'

The touch of Quinn's hands on hers was doing

strange things to her. Fern pulled back again but his hold only tightened.

'I'm starting to think you don't even know what passion is...' Quinn was almost talking to himself. '"There's more to life than passion,"' he repeated. 'Good grief, woman...'

'There is!'

'There might be,' Quinn agreed, 'but it sure as heaven helps life along. If you can find someone who makes you feel...'

'Feel what?' Fern was past lowering her voice now. She was just plain angry and this man holding her was making her feel torn in two. 'I don't know what you're talking about.'

Quinn's deep eyes darkened. For one more moment he stood looking down at her in the warm night air and then he swore softly to himself.

'I dare say I'll regret this in the morning,' he muttered savagely. 'But it's time to show—not tell!'

And he pulled her to him in one swift, effortless movement. His mouth lowered to hers and in the next instant Fern was being ruthlessly kissed.

She should have struggled.

Of course she should have struggled. She didn't want this man to kiss her. She didn't...

Fern could never tell afterwards if she lifted her face at the critical moment. She could never tell if she had expected—wanted—what happened as Quinn's mouth met hers.

All she knew was that some weird feeling was sweeping through her—something connected with the warmth of this man's strong hands and the feel of his mouth brushing her lips.

Brushing?

The kiss was a gentle brush for only a moment—a feather kiss of a question while she stood still and mute and unable to draw away.

Unable or unwilling?

Who could say? Certainly not Fern Rycroft.

It was like surgical cases Fern had read of where only one anaesthetic took hold during an operation—the anaesthetic that paralysed the body and yet kept every sense still tingling with awareness. Able to feel every pinprick of pain.

Yet this wasn't pain. The lightness of the kiss had faded. Something deeper was happening here. Something she didn't understand and had no control over.

Quinn's hands had released her fingers and were now around her waist, circling her slender body and pulling her in against his hard, muscled thighs. His lips had stopped their gentle searching. They had moved from gentleness to straight plunder in one savage instant.

And she was responding.

Dear heaven, she could feel herself responding. Fern felt her lips open for him to deepen the kiss, compelled by a force that was stronger than anything she had felt before.

He was so. . .

So. . .

So male!

The word drifted through her overwhelmed senses as the only way she could describe him. What was drawing her to him seemed something she had no control over—Eve to Adam. . . Woman to Man—a primeval, aching need that had nothing to do with sense or responsibility or future security. . .

No!

From somewhere—somewhere so far back in the recesses of her mind that it was almost lost, Fern found the last vestige of common sense reasserting itself.

She shoved her hands against Quinn Gallagher's chest and shoved as hard as she could.

She was released and she knew, as his lips left hers and she staggered back from him, that the only thing her traitorous body felt was regret.

'What. . .what the heck do you think you're doing?' Her breath was coming in panting gasps.

'Not *me*...' he said and, like Fern, Quinn's voice was shaken to the depths.

He made no move to follow her. Quinn Gallagher stood looking down at Fern in the filtered moonlight and his dark eyes were enigmatic and fathoms deep. 'We, Fern Rycroft,' he corrected her gently. 'I believe *we* were engaged in a spot of passion. Something you don't believe in.'

'No!' It was a cry from the heart. Fern put her hands to her lips as if she could wipe away his touch. 'I didn't...'

'Didn't want it?' Quinn's mouth quirked. 'Liar.'

'I'm not.'

'Can your Sam make you feel like that?' Quinn shook his head. He stepped forward and his hand came out to touch her face lightly.

Fern flinched and backed still further.

'I'm going... I'm going back in to Aunt Maud,' she whispered.

Quinn nodded. 'I think that's wise,' he told her gently. 'Run to your aunt. But, Fern...'

'Y-yes?'

'Surely an almost married lady should run to her intended? Unless...unless her intended was never that in the first place.'

CHAPTER FOUR

THERE was no danger of Fern going to sleep after that. She lay staring at moonbeams on the ceiling and her mind twisted on a tortuous path she had no way of escaping. The fact that Aunt Maud's pulse beat strongly and regularly under Fern's fingers hardly made her feel better at all.

It was a real relief when morning came.

At six the ward door opened and a middle-aged lady appeared, bearing a tray. Fern recognized her at once. Geraldine Hamstead, a near neighbour of Fern's aunt and uncle and one of the island's few trained nurses.

'Cup of tea?' Geraldine whispered cheerfully, and bent to check Maud. 'Oh, she's still sleeping...'

As if to give the lie to the statement, Maud's eyes flicked open. Maud stared up at Geraldine and then looked across at Fern in bewilderment.

'Geraldine... Fern...' And then the events of the previous day flooded back and Maud's face crumpled into tears.

'Oh, Fern, your lovely wedding. Oh, Fern...'

'Now, you're not to fret yourself over a silly wedding, Auntie,' Fern said soundly, slipping from her own bedcovers to give her aunt a swift hug. There were still monitors attached to Maud's breast and a saline drip was attached to her arm but it was more important to hug the elderly lady at this stage than to worry about leads and tubing. 'I can get married any old day,' Fern smiled.

'But not on the island. I know you won't get married on the island after this.' Fern's aunt gulped back tears. 'It was Lizzy, wasn't it?'

'Yes,' Fern agreed. 'We might have known she'd do something silly. Forget her now, though, Aunt. What's done is done and Geraldine has a good strong cup of tea here that needs drinking. Do you feel like it?'

'Y-yes, please...'

There were still weak tears sliding down Maud's face. She struggled to sit up but Geraldine and Fern were there before her, sliding their arms in behind, supporting her and helping her to hold the cup as she sipped.

'You shouldn't have to do this, Geraldine... Fern...' Maud whispered as, tea finished, she sank gratefully back onto her pillows.

'My pleasure.' Geraldine smiled fondly down at her neighbour. 'I should have been here last night but I was so darned crook with those dratted oysters! So was Barbara and we're the only two trained nurses on the island free to help at the hospital. It was a blessing Doc Gallagher and Jess didn't go to your wedding lunch, too. Now...' Geraldine turned her starched smile onto Fern '...I'm intending to give your aunt a wash, Fern Rycroft, so be off with you and let us get on with it. Dr Gallagher wants a word.'

A word...

She had to face him some time. Fern would have liked to slink off home and reappear in about a year. She didn't feel up to facing Quinn Gallagher yet.

Geraldine had turned to fill a bowl with warm water from the basin on the wall. Smiling still, she jerked her head to the door.

'Doc Gallagher's a busy man, Fern,' she warned. 'I wouldn't keep the good doctor waiting. He's in the office down the corridor to your left. And don't worry,' she added, seeing Fern's hesitation and misreading the reason, 'your aunt's in good hands.'

Fern threw up her hands in mock surrender and managed a smile. 'OK, OK. I know when I'm not wanted.'

Quinn was waiting for her. He was sipping black tea from a huge chipped mug and he gestured to a teapot the size of which Fern had never seen in her life. It was vast.

'Now I know how you keep yourself awake,' she told him, only just containing the tremor in her voice.

'Beats amphetamines.' Quinn rose from his desk and looked quizzically down at Fern. 'I told you, I'm used to sleep deprivation—but you look dead beat.'

'I hardly had a restful night,' Fern said bitterly and then wished she hadn't.

'Is that tone of voice inferring that you had a restless night because of me?' Quinn's eyebrows rose in polite incredulity.

'You didn't help.'

'Dr Rycroft, I hardly think you're fitted for married life if a fleeting kiss can be described as disturbing.'

'"Fleeting"...' Fern's breath was dragged in as a gasp of outrage.

'OK.' Quinn spread his hands placatingly. 'It wasn't fleeting. It was, in fact, most satisfactory. Would you care for a repeat performance?'

'I would not!' Fern backed like a frightened rabbit.

'Pity.' Quinn's dark eyes gleamed with dangerous humour. He didn't pursue it, though, but sighed in mock resignation. 'Never mind. There's time to spare. How about if I keep dreamboat chained to his bed for weeks while I have my wicked way with you?'

'If you mean Sam...'

'But of course I mean Sam.' Quinn's eyes widened in innocence. 'How many dreamboats do you have, Dr Rycroft?'

It was all Fern could do not to slap his smiling face. The man laughed down at her with warmth and admiration in his eyes and she felt her world shift crazily on its axis. She was badly out of control and she knew it.

'You...you wanted to see me?' she asked stiffly.

'I certainly did.' Quinn's innocent gaze gave way to laughter once again. 'For a lady who's slept in her clothes you've come up looking remarkably presentable, I must say.' He leaned forward and smoothed down an errant flaming curl wisping over her forehead. 'Even cute!'

'I am not cute!' Fern was perilously close to stamping her foot. She fought frantically for dignity and control and somehow found it.

'OK, then,' Quinn agreed. 'Not cute.' His smile faded. 'Let's make that efficient and professional and businesslike, shall we, Dr Rycroft? Tell me what you're going to do about your aunt.'

Fern stared. 'Why. . .? What do you mean?'

'She won't go to the city,' he told her. 'We had that out long before she had this heart attack. She has no intention of seeing a specialist anywhere but on this island. She says that the stress of travelling to Sydney and putting herself through all those "damned fool tests" would be the death of her—and she may even be right, at that. She has severe ischaemic heart disease, Dr Rycroft.'

The anger drained from Fern in a sickening rush. She groped for the back of a chair and sat down hard.

'How. . .how bad?'

'You want to see the ECG?' Without waiting for an answer Quinn reached back to his desk and produced the tracing. He handed it to Fern without a word.

Fern studied it in silence. Above their heads a clock ticked with monotonous regularity. Like a time bomb. . .

'This ECG was taken last week,' Quinn told Fern as she laid the tape down. 'She's been seeing me on and off for chest pain and I've been doing my damnedest to keep things under control. Your fiasco with the wedding from hell was too much, though. Heaven knows what the ECG will look like now. She'll have suffered considerably more damage after last night.'

'I didn't know it was this bad. . .'

'Because you haven't been home.'

'I guess. . .I guess that's right.' Fern thought back to all those cheerful letters she'd received from her aunt—with never a hint that there were problems. Her uncle's letters were few and far between——but Fern remembered now a couple of phone calls that had sounded stilted and absurdly formal. She'd guessed that he was worried but, when pressed, Al had just passed it off as concern over a heifer or a fence needing urgent repair down in the bottom paddock.

'So, what do you intend to do about it?'

'"Do"?' Fern stared. She picked up the tape again and looked along its length, willing it to tell her something different. 'I don't know...'

'She's a candidate for a bypass.'

'She won't go to Sydney for it,' Fern said definitely. Then she frowned and stared again at the tape. 'How do you know a bypass would help?'

'I ran tests myself and sent the results to Sydney. A friend of mine's a heart specialist there. He says he's willing to book her in for angiography and probable bypass on the strength of my information.'

'But...'

'But she won't go without your persuasion,' Quinn said. 'And if she stays here...Well, if she stays here without the operation I reckon she'll be lucky if she lives twelve months.'

'I'll try and persuade her,' Fern said miserably, knowing that her chances of doing any such thing were zero. Her aunt had been off the island once when she was ten. She'd been seasick and homesick in equal proportions. The thought of aeroplanes made her almost sick with horror and nothing could persuade her to repeat the experience.

'And if you can't?'

Fern fingered the tape. 'There's nothing...'

'You could stay with her.'

'It won't help,' Fern said miserably. 'It won't make her live longer.'

'No.' Quinn's voice softened. 'It won't.' He reached out and took the tape from Fern's fingers and then his strong hands clasped hers together and held them still. Quinn wasn't talking to her as another doctor. He was talking to her as a frightened relative who had to be made to face facts.

'But your uncle's not strong enough to cope with his wife's death alone, Fern, and I've checked. You're his only family. You're all he has, Dr Rycroft, and your place, for the next twelve months or however long it takes, is within easy reach of the people who love you.'

'But. . .but I can't come back. I can't stay here.' It was a frightened wail.

'Why not?'

'Sam. . .' Fern's mind was twisting like a cornered animal, searching for a way of escape. 'I'm marrying Sam and Sam won't stay. . .'

'Sam doesn't love you,' Quinn said brutally. 'That bag of wind has a heart only big enough for himself.'

'That's not fair. He. . .'

'Dr Rycroft, why don't you want to come back to the island?'

Quinn's flat demand cut across Fern's rising panic. It stopped her almost in mid-flight.

There was a long, long silence.

'It's almost as if you're afraid,' Quinn said slowly. 'Of what, I wonder?'

'I'm not. . . Don't be ridiculous. . .'

'I'm not being ridiculous.' Quinn's dark eyes were searching her face, seeking clues behind her shadowed eyes.

'Your aunt tells me you lost your parents,' he said gently. He ignored Fern's gasp and her sharp tug on her hands and went on as though thinking aloud. 'You lost your parents and your sister in the one dreadful car crash. It must have been hard to take for a kid of fifteen.'

'Look, it's. . .'

'None of my business?' Quinn finished for her. 'I know. But I'm starting to guess all the same, Fern Rycroft. Would I be right in believing you've made a personal vow never to leave yourself so exposed again? Never to admit to loving? Because if you admit to loving then you face the risk of that awful pain again.'

'No. . .'

'Is that why you're scared to death of staying any nearer Al and Maud than you have to? Of staying on the island where people are fond of you? And is that why you're marrying that bag of wind? So you can have safety and security without the risk of pain if he leaves you?'

'You don't know what you're talking about!' Fern wrenched futilely at her hands. Her green eyes were flashing daggers. The man was so right that it hurt—and yet he was saying things that she'd hardly admitted to herself. 'No!'

'I'm right, aren't I, Dr Rycroft?' Quinn asked gently. His clasp on her hands tightened, as though he was trying to impart strength for what she had to do. 'But there's a responsibility you can't escape from, my lovely Fern. Your aunt and uncle love you, regardless, and they need you. Your place is here.'

My lovely Fern.

The words twisted deep down into Fern's heart and pierced like a blade. There was pain coming at her from all sides and some of it was to do with the way she felt about the man holding her hands.

She wrenched again.

'Let me go. I don't have to listen to this.'

'You have to face it.'

'I couldn't stay here even if I wanted to,' Fern snapped. 'There's no room on the island for more than one doctor—and I'd hate to do you out of a job.'

'I'd hate you to do me out of a job, too,' Quinn said thoughtfully. He was still holding her hands in a grip of iron but it was almost as though he had forgotten that he was holding them. 'So, what do we do about that?'

'Nothing!'

'I'd be prepared to offer you a partnership.'

A partnership.

Fern stared at the man before her as if he had finally

lost his head. He stared right back and his eyes were as calm as a safe harbour after a storm.

His hands were still holding hers. She stared down at them and, seemingly reluctantly, Quinn released her.

'It could work,' he said gently.

'The island's not big enough.'

'It is, you know,' he told her. 'The township's growing and there are plans for a two-hundred-bed hotel on the foreshore. The local airline has applied for a licence to increase its runs and with tourists there's a huge increase in workload. I didn't come here to be run off my feet—so I'll need help. Now I have an established service I'll advertise on the mainland—but I'd prefer an islander. I'd prefer you.'

'Why did you come here?' Fern asked abruptly.

Quinn just smiled and shook his head. He lifted a hand to run his fingers through his already tousled hair. 'It doesn't make any difference why I came. The point is that I'm here; I intend to stay for quite a while; I'd like to make this the best medical practice I possibly can afford to provide; and I have on the island a qualified doctor with inside knowledge of every one of the islanders. I'd be a fool to pass you over, Dr Rycroft.'

His laughing eyes were saying more than that and Fern flushed crimson.

'I don't want to be your partner, Dr Gallagher,' she snapped and her voice dripped ice.

'Why ever not?' That dangerous innocence flashed out again and Fern was lost.

'I...I don't...' She fought for breath and dragged herself to her feet. This was getting way out of hand. 'Look, it's a great offer and I appreciate it. But my life—my plans—have nothing to do with you and I'll thank you to butt out. Now...'

'Now what?'

'Now I'm going home to have breakfast,' she snapped.

'It's already cooked.' Quinn followed her to his feet, his long body stretching lazily. 'Heck, morning already.' He glanced down at his watch. 'Seven a.m. and I can smell bacon. Come and see what Jessie is cooking.'

'I don't want breakfast.'

'You mean you don't mind offending Jessie?' He smiled down at her. 'She's done the right thing by helping with your aunt; she's cooked you breakfast and now you're going to leave without even tasting it. I don't know where you were raised, Dr Rycroft, but where I was brought up that would have been classed as bad manners. Almost up there with belching in public or being seen with your hair in curlers.'

'I'm not...' Fern fought for dignity but lost it somewhere between tears and laughter. 'Oh, for heaven's sake...You're blackmailing me.'

'That's the plan,' he said easily. He took her hands in a grip that brooked no protest. 'Breakfast, Dr Rycroft,' he said firmly. 'A woman can't consider the best offer she's had in years on an empty stomach.'

Jessie wasn't in the kitchen.

She'd hardly have known if Fern had eaten her breakfast. The back door was swinging shut as they walked through from the corridor and the pan of bacon sizzled untended on the stove.

A note lay on the table.

Didn't like to disturb what was obviously a tête-à-tête. One of Chris Ming's horses sounds like he's broken his hock. Gotta go. Hi, Fern. Quinn, could you feed Walter? Leave me a bit of bacon. I'll eat it cold.

There was enough bacon to feed a small army. Fern stood by the door and stared as Quinn walked over to the stove and started flipping it over.

'You do share...' she started cautiously. The relationship between Quinn and Jessie was unexplained. If it wasn't for Quinn's kiss last night she would have guessed they were married.

'We have separate kitchens,' Quinn told her, seeing her doubt. 'Separate everything, in fact. It's only Jessie's cooking that drives me in here. Finally, she's taken pity on me and feeds me—as long as I help look after her babies.'

'Babies?'

'Walter,' Quinn grinned. 'Well, Walter for one.' He leaned over beside the stove and lifted a small woollen pouch that had been hanging behind a chair. An electric cord looped out from the pouch and ran to a nearby socket.

'Would you like to meet Walter, Dr Rycroft?' he asked, and held open the pouch.

It was another wallaby—but a little one only half the size of the joey Fern had met the night before. It was still pink, its skin only slightly fuzzed with the beginnings of soft brown fur.

'Walter's mum was burned when one of the local farmers lost control of a burn-off,' Quinn explained. 'Jess had to put the mum down and the little one darn near died as well. He was suffering smoke inhalation and even without it at that age they're hard to keep alive.'

Quinn abandoned the bacon, handed the pouch to Fern and crossed to the fridge. On the top shelf were a series of what looked like doll's bottles—bottles Fern had only seen before being used to feed very premature babies. 'Sit down,' he told Fern. 'You can feed the baby while I finish breakfast. Fair division of labour.'

'I don't know how. . .' Fern peered dubiously into the bag. Lining the pouch was a tiny electric blanket, making a cocoon of warmth to imitate the mother's pouch. From the depths peered two tiny eyes and they looked just as anxious as Fern's did.

'Nothing to it.' Quinn grinned. 'Jess makes me do it and if I can do it then anyone can.' He heated the bottle in the microwave, retrieved a piece of blanket from the warming drawer of the oven and brought both to Fern.

'Sit,' he said sternly and, slightly stunned, Fern sat.

Quinn laid the blanket on Fern's lap and then, with fingers that looked as though they were handling a rare and precious piece of antiquity, he delved into the pouch and retrieved the baby wallaby. In seconds he had wrapped the tiny creature like a newborn infant so that it was lying on its back, its nose pointing up at Fern.

Fern had never met a man so gentle.

Quinn dripped a droplet of milk onto the inside of his wrist, checked it again and then lowered the bottle. The joey saw it coming. The tiny mouth opened in anticipation, the extended teat went down the little throat and he started to suck.

Fern stared down in amazement.

Her arms instinctively cradled her warm little bundle and she took the bottle from Quinn. Despite herself, her lips curved into a soft smile.

'Jess does this all the time?'

'*We* do this,' Quinn grinned. 'Now Jess has decided I'm trustworthy I get to share two-hourly feeds. You see why I'd like you to join the medical practice of Barega?'

Fern shook her head but her attention was all on the tiny mouth and those huge, trusting eyes, watching her...

'I've never seen a wallaby so tiny...'

'He isn't due to leave the pouch for months yet,' Quinn told her, turning back to the bacon. 'Toast?'

'Oh... Yes...'

'Mind, it's too early to say whether he ever will.' Quinn held a piece of bacon up with tongs. 'Will this do or do you like it crisp?'

'Whatever...' Fern had more on her mind than bacon.

'Crisp, then,' Quinn said definitely. 'There's nothing worse than soggy bacon, in my book.'

'Why may he never leave the pouch?' Fern asked

cautiously. The soft warm bundle in her arms, Fern's lack of sleep and the smells wafting round the kitchen were causing her mind almost to be disembodied. She felt as if she was floating slightly above where her body was sitting.

'They're deuced hard to raise,' Quinn told her. 'Even now we're not out of the woods with this one. Jess carried the joey round in a pouch against her body for the first couple of weeks after we found him. The stress of being away from the movement and smell of the mother kills them quicker than anything else does. I couldn't believe the trouble she went to. The joey even went to bed with her. Then we tried one antibiotic after another to get rid of the infection in the lung—it's not completely clear yet—and we had an impossible time finding a formula that'd suit.'

'We. . .'

Quinn grinned. 'Well, it's hard to stay completely divorced from proceedings. I use Jess for anything from holding a stroppy kid down while I check an ear to giving an anaesthetic in an emergency, and she responds by dabbling in my pharmacy cupboard as well as hers. In a restricted place like this there's no such thing as total separation of animal medicine and people medicine.'

'I see,' Fern said faintly.

Quinn grinned. 'A far cry from a city teaching hospital,' he smiled. 'Why don't you join us and see how much fun it can be?'

Fun. . . Medicine, fun?

Fern had always taken her work so seriously—a way to escape the fears that had been with her for so long. The thought of medicine as fun was almost an anathema.

Yet. . .

She looked around this warm, cluttered kitchen and the thought of being part of it was so tempting that it was almost irresistible.

She looked up to find Quinn's eyes watching her, his face creased with laughing understanding.

'You could do it, you know,' he said kindly. 'It's like jumping off the high board into a swimming pool on a hot day. So scary it makes your knees wobble but if you hold your nose and do it... Well, it's a lot more comfortable in the water than staying for ever on the high board.'

Is that what she was doing? Staying for ever on the high board?

By marrying Sam, maybe she was. Maybe her knees were trembling almost as much now at the thought of marrying Sam and leaving...

Dear heaven, where was her traitorous mind leading her? She had her life all mapped out. A husband. A job. When she returned to the mainland she was completing her training as a physician. A financially secure career in a huge hospital where she didn't need to become close to people...

In her arms the little wallaby stirred and settled and his bright eyes closed in sleep. She could feel his tummy swollen with milk and for one absurd moment she had a vision that was totally crazy.

This man...this fireside, only instead of a joey a human baby—a baby with eyes the same as his father's...

Well, that was one stupid, stupid thought. Fern gave herself a sharp mental kick. She lifted the empty bottle from the unresponsive mouth and knelt to place the joey back in his warm little pouch. No children! Sam agreed. They'd be in the way of his career path, he said, and they were certainly in the way of Fern's need for no ties.

She stood stiffly, her eyes blank with fear. She was getting into deeper and deeper water and she wanted out.

'Bathroom's next door,' Quinn said kindly, seeing her confusion and obviously deciding not to make it worse. 'Have a wash while I do the eggs. Sunny side up?'

'Y-yes, please.'

He smiled at her, his eyes sending out a message of reassurance as though he could read her fear.

'Two minutes, then, Dr Rycroft. Or I'll wolf the lot without you.'

CHAPTER FIVE

IT WAS a weird breakfast.

Fern spent the meal trying to shake off the feeling that she belonged in this kitchen.

She felt as if she'd been here all her life.

It was crazy. Aunt Maud kept her kitchen as neat as a new pin and Fern's hospital flat was clinically clean and uncluttered. No photographs. No sentimentality or memorabilia at all.

It was different here. The kitchen was vast. The centre point was a huge slow combustion stove that almost filled a wall and sent out a soft heat into the slight chill of the morning. The stove seemed the kitchen's heart.

Around them was the semi-organised clutter of two professionals' busy lives. There were not nearly enough shelves to hold all the different sorts of feed mixtures Jessie seemed to need. Bags of formula stood heaped along one wall and more were stacked by the stove. To complete the impression of confusion, from the ceiling someone had hung lavender. Maybe a hundred or more bunches were suspended to dry.

'Jess loves the smell.' Quinn smiled. 'And I don't object too much either.' He motioned across at the open window to the sea beyond. 'Especially when it's mixed with the salt from the ocean.'

There was the smell of more than lavender and salt—and bacon. A bright mound of cut fuchsias and roses tumbled in disarray on the floor, giving off a heady scent of their own.

Maybe Jess had cut them before going out and had not had time to put them in vases, Fern decided—and then blinked as a tiny wombat burrowed out from its pouch somewhere behind her and snuffled over to chomp at the pile.

Fern thought the flowers beautiful. The wombat thought them delicious.

'How...how many animals does Jessie have here?' Fern asked faintly and Quinn shook his head.

'Too many.' He smiled ruefully. 'She has four littlies inside at the moment—the wallaby, this little wombat, a baby rosella she puts on the verandah during the day and there's an echidna behind the stove...'

'An echidna...' Australia's answer to the English porcupine. 'How...how cuddly!'

'He is cuddly, too,' Quinn smiled. 'Did you know they don't grow spikes till they're twelve months old? Jess feeds him herself, thank heaven. Porcupines don't use teats—they knead their mother's belly and the milk oozes onto the surface for the baby to lick off. Feeding Oscar is therefore a messy business.'

'R-really?'

Quinn grinned. 'Shame on you, Dr Rycroft. What do they teach in paediatric medicine these days? Didn't you know that?'

'N-no.' Fern's feeling of unreality was growing and growing.

'Oscar's the most frail of the babies here so I won't take him out of his warm pouch for show and tell,' Quinn told her. 'Jess has had a hard time settling his diarrhoea. With luck, next time you eat breakfast here it'll be feed time.'

'I won't...'

'Be eating with us again?' Quinn raised disbelieving eyebrows. 'You know, I'm very sure you will.' He smiled. 'Very sure, Fern Rycroft. Coffee?'

'What, have you emptied your teapot?' Fern quizzed in an unsteady effort to lighten what she was feeling.

'I have coffee twice a day to wash the tea down.' Quinn grinned. His smile faded. 'Dr Rycroft, this partnership is a serious offer, you know. I'm sure we could work together and your aunt tells me you've done an anaesthetic residency. I'm a surgeon, so...'

'A surgeon!' Fern's eyes widened. So she had been right. 'But...'

'But I've also specialised in emergency medicine.' He saw the blatant disbelief in her eyes. 'So... So, together we could provide a damned good service...'

'But I don't know why you came...'

Fern's tone was almost an accusation—as though consideration of his offer was dependent on her knowing his reasons for being on the island.

'No.' Quinn nodded, his face thoughtful. 'You don't. But I had my reasons and they're good ones. Sometimes you just have to take people on trust, Dr Rycroft.'

'But...' Fern stared at Quinn, baffled, and then tried a sideways tack.

'OK,' she said at last. 'Jessie must have come at the same time as you. Why did she come to the island?'

Quinn's face cleared. 'Well, that's easy,' he grinned. 'Jessie came here because cats are banned from the island, foxes don't exist and even rats haven't made their way to the island yet. It's a wildlife utopia, and Jess has been looking for such a place all her life.'

'You mean she came here because of her animals?'

'Jess is a vet, Fern.' Quinn's face grew thoughtful. 'She loves her animals—and maybe, like you, Jess has cut herself off from people. She's one of the few registered carers in the state allowed to both actively treat injured wildlife and then keep them to release. On the mainland she has to send them to bush shelters after treatment because there's nowhere round the city where they can safely be released. Here...'

'There are still dogs.'

'That's where our Jess is a resourceful lady.' Quinn smiled. 'She knew the island wanted a vet so she wrote with a few conditions when she offered to come. One is that all dogs—no exceptions—are carefully controlled and kept confined after dark and that rule is rigidly policed. The farmers here are so pleased to have a qualified vet they'd have granted her the moon. Keeping their dogs under control seemed easy in comparison.'

'I—I see. . .'

Fern put down her half-finished coffee and stared at the floor. She couldn't meet those eyes.

'So, what do you say, Fern?' Quinn asked gently. 'Will you join us?'

Fern shook her head.

'Because the high board's too far up from the water?' Quinn reached out and tucked a curl back behind Fern's ear. 'Maybe I'd be below waiting to catch. . . And maybe, just maybe, the water wouldn't be too cold after all. . . It's feeling pretty warm from where I stand.'

The silence grew. Fern felt the colour grow from white to fiery pink and back to white again.

Quinn withdrew his hand from her hair. He didn't touch her again and she didn't know whether she wished him to or not.

'I have to go. . .' she said finally and he nodded.

'I guess you do.' Then, at her look of surprise, Quinn glanced ruefully at his watch. 'I have a clinic at nine and a ward round to do that's almost respectably long this morning so, much as I'd like to, I can't keep looking at you and turning my thoughts from medicine. Will you have dinner with me tonight?'

The invitation caught her by surprise.

'No!' It was a whisper of defiance. Fern stood abruptly and backed a foot toward the door.

'How uncivil!' Quinn shook his head but his dark eyes kept smiling. 'My cooking's not that bad,' he said plaintively. 'Will you reconsider if I ask Jess to cook?'

Fern backed another foot. 'It's. . .it's very kind of you—of you and Jess—but I'll have dinner with my uncle. I. . .I only intend to stay on the island for another couple of days so I should spend all the time I can with. . .with my family.'

'OK, Fern.' Quinn rose, stepped forward and brushed her cheek lightly with one finger, the smile fading for an instant. 'You do that. But in the next couple of days you'd better start believing that Al and Maud are your family. They love you already, Fern, no matter how hard you hold yourself away from them; and there are more people around than just your aunt and Al who could love you—given half a chance.'

'Don't. . .'

She pushed his hand away in confusion and turned to the door.

'I won't,' Quinn said softly as she disappeared fast down the corridor. 'At least, not yet. . .'

Fern visited her aunt before she left and found Maud almost asleep again, her face devoid of colour against the pillows. She turned to the door as Fern entered and gave a tremulous smile.

Fern crossed swiftly, her heart jerking within at her aunt's obvious frailty.

'Oh, Aunt. . .' She stopped to give her a swift hug. 'Why didn't you tell me about your heart? You should never have tried to cope with the wedding. If only I'd known. . .'

'If you'd known it would have been a glorious excuse to have your wedding in some dingy registry office on the mainland,' her aunt whispered and managed to smile. 'Go on, Fern. Admit it.'

'It wouldn't have been an excuse.' Fern sat on the chair beside the bed and took her aunt's hand. 'But I should have noticed things weren't right when I finally did come home.' She sighed. 'Aunt, Dr Gallagher says you could be a candidate for a bypass operation—and a bypass could just save your life.'

'What does he know?' Maud's lips compressed into a tight line.

'He knows what's best for you,' Fern told her. 'Auntie Maud, you're an otherwise fit woman. You're just sixty. You could have twenty or thirty good years if you have the operation.'

'He can't do it here.'

'Well, no,' Fern admitted. Coronary bypasses needed a team of skilled coronary surgeons and specially trained nurses. Such surgery on Barega was unthinkable.

'So I'd have to go to Sydney?'

'Yes.' There was no point in dissembling. 'But I'd go with you. I'd stay with you all the time.'

'And afterwards?'

'I'd bring you home to Barega. I promise.'

'And then go back to Sydney?'

'I must, Aunt,' Fern said gently. 'Sydney's my home.'

'No, it's not,' Maud said sadly. 'Nowhere's home. Not since your family died. You've never let this place be home and even when you marry Sam, Sydney will be just the place where you both get on with your careers. It won't be home.'

'Aunt, we shouldn't be worrying about me,' Fern said gently. 'We're talking about you—and about the probability of more heart attacks unless you do something about it.'

'I'm not going. . .'

'You don't think that's a little selfish?' Fern tried, watching her aunt's face. 'Aunt, I don't know how my uncle will cope without you and that's the truth.'

'He'll have to.'

'Do you want him to?'

Silence.

'No,' Maud said at last. 'Of course I don't.' She twisted in the bed and looked at Fern. 'It was just so awful last time I went. . .'

'Last time was fifty years ago,' Fern said with

asperity. 'Last time your parents put you on a fishing boat in bad weather and it took a week to get to the mainland. Aunt, we can do better than that. We could even get a specially equipped hospital plane to land and transport you...'

'A plane? One of those noisy tin cans that fall out of the sky...'

'Believe it or not, they fall out of the sky once in a blue moon and I've been watching carefully of late. The moon's not blue at all,' Fern said. 'You'd be surprised how comfortable they are now.'

'My father went on a joyride once. He was green for weeks.'

'That was forty years ago. Aunt, aviation has come a long way since then.'

'I...'

'Auntie Maud, you know you can get through this if you set your mind to it,' Fern whispered, laying her cheek against her aunt's. 'Do it for my uncle. And for me. Please?'

'For you...' Aunt Maud's hand came up to clasp Fern's soft chestnut curls. 'Oh, Fern, you don't need me. You never have.'

'I do.'

'I wish that was true. But...' A tear slid down Maud's face. She closed her eyes. 'Fern, you won't even get married on the island now, will you?'

'We'd be silly to,' Fern whispered.

'You mean you have a good excuse.' Maud shook her head and her lips tightened. There was a long moment's silence while she thought. Then her eyes flashed open again.

'Fern, I still want you to marry on the island. Drat Lizzy and her tricks. I'm asking you to try again.'

'But...'

'No buts,' her aunt said sternly, her voice strengthening with decision. 'I'll do you a deal.'

'What...what sort of deal?'

'If you promise to marry on the island then I'll have

this darned operation. Bring on your hospital planes, your helicopters... Bring on the army for all I care. I want to see you married, Fern, dear, and I want you to be married among your own. I want you to be married here. So... So is it a deal?'

Another island wedding? To go through with all this tomfoolery again? Every nerve in Fern's body rebelled against the thought.

'But Sam...'

'Sam will marry here if you want to badly enough.'

'I don't think...'

'You can persuade him, if you try.'

Maybe she could. The problem was that Fern wasn't too sure she wanted to persuade anybody.

'Aunt...'

Fern's words broke off mid-sentence as the door opened behind them and Quinn Gallagher walked in.

'I need to check your aunt before Clinic,' Quinn said apologetically to Fern. He smiled down at Maud. 'I suppose you haven't changed your mind about this operation?'

'I have and all,' Maud whispered triumphantly, her eyes only just a little bit scared. 'Tell him, Fern.'

'She says she'll go,' Fern said faintly.

'But tell him your promise,' Maud demanded. 'So you've made it in front of witnesses. If I die in the next five minutes your promise is still binding.'

'I've promised my aunt that if she agrees to the operation then I'll marry on the island.' Fern's voice was almost as weak a whisper as her aunt's.

'Marry Sam?' Quinn's expressive eyebrows rose skyward.

'I don't care if Fern changes her mind and marries the local undertaker,' Maud muttered. She'd had her win and fatigue was starting to show. 'But whoever she marries, she marries here. Right, Fern?'

'R-right.'

'Well, well,' Quinn Gallagher drawled. He looked

down at Fern and his mouth quirked into an enigmatic smile. 'Well, well. . .'

Good grief. . .

What on earth had she done? Made promises that she had no way of knowing she could keep?

Fern left Maud to Quinn Gallagher's capable care and escaped to the corridor.

Sam. . . She should see Sam before she went back to her uncle's. He'd expect a visit for sure.

Why didn't she want to see him?

She opened his door with trepidation, expecting maybe a repeat of the tirade of last night. Instead of scowls, however, Sam was sitting up in bed looking perfectly resplendent in his purple pyjamas and beaming with his usual good humour.

Sam normally was benign and happy, Fern thought. It was only the shock of being ill that had thrown him.

'Fern. . .' Sam held out his hands and Fern had no choice but to walk across to the bed and take them. He kissed her soundly on both cheeks. 'How are you, sweetheart? And how's your aunt?'

'She's better this morning,' Fern told him, managing a smile to match his. 'But still very weak.'

Sam took a deep breath. Clearly something was disturbing him. 'Fern, Dr Gallagher told me this morning just how close to death she'd been—and he also told me I was a right twit last night. Will you forgive me?'

The wind was knocked out of Fern's sails in a rush. She looked down at Sam and saw the same kid she'd grown up with—the man she was as familiar with as a pair of old socks—and the reasons she was marrying him firmed back to solid comfort.

'You were frightened yourself,' she reassured him. 'I was just grateful I didn't eat any of those dreadful oysters myself.'

'I didn't think Lizzy would go that far for me,' Sam said, and his tone was half-admiring. 'She's quite a girl.'

'Sam...' Fern pulled back and stared at her fiancé in concern. 'Sam, are you absolutely sure you don't want to marry Lizzy?'

'Marry...' Sam's face froze. 'No. Of course not. What on earth put that idea into your head? Fern, you know that thing we had in the past is well and truly over—at least it is with me. Sure, we were a pair when we were kids—but that was before you came, and before I decided I wanted a life off the island. What sort of lawyer's wife do you reckon Lizzy would make? First, she'd be scared stiff to leave here and second... well, imagine asking clients home to dinner. If she didn't like them I'd have to taste test their food for poison.'

'She wouldn't do that,' Fern said slowly. 'Sam, if Lizzy conformed a bit more... Are you saying you'd just as soon marry her as me?'

Sam smiled and shook his head, his hands still holding Fern's.

'Of course not, Fern. I want a sensible wife—not a scatterbrain. You had a bad day, sweetheart, and it's making you have doubts. Most brides have nerves before the wedding.'

'But...'

'Fern, we've agreed this is a really sensible choice. We know each other so well there are no surprises. We don't fight. We both want careers without children and neither of us believe in this crazy thing called romance. So... We're made for each other, Fern, and you know it. So as soon as we get back to Sydney...'

'Aunt Maud wants us to marry here. Still...'

Sam frowned. 'But Lizzy...'

'I don't think Lizzy will interfere again,' Fern said sadly, thinking of Lizzy's half scared, half defiant face as she'd left her yesterday. 'I think it would be kinder to Lizzy if we married elsewhere—but my aunt's desperate to see us married. She says if we marry here she'll come to the mainland with us and have a bypass operation—and she needs it if she's to live.'

'Your aunt leave the island. . .' Sam lay back on his pillows and stared up at Fern in amazement. He knew Maud almost as well as Fern did and he knew what a concession she was making. 'Whew. . .'

'So you see. . .'

'Yeah, I see.' Sam stroked his smooth chin thoughtfully. 'Well, we've three weeks' honeymoon and today's only Sunday. How about if we marry on Friday? It still gives us two weeks' study time back in Sydney before we start work.'

Just like that. As romantic as making a pot of tea. . . Quinn's tea. . .

Stop thinking about the man. Fern forced her mind back to practicalities with a mammoth effort.

'O-OK. A small wedding, though, Sam. Maybe even here if my aunt's not well enough to come to church. Just my aunt and uncle and your parents.'

'Suits me.' He smiled. 'Even Lizzy won't dare try anything if we're marrying in the hospital. But you'll still wear your gorgeous dress, won't you, Fern? You looked smashing.'

Fern thought back to the crumpled mound of soiled wedding dress she had left lying on her bedroom floor. Ugh. . .

'I'll have to have it cleaned,' she said reluctantly. Why was her major impulse to bury the dress and be done with it? 'But, yes, I'll wear the dress.'

'Then that's settled. . .'

'And I'm staying in hospital till then,' Frank Reid hooted from behind the curtain. He'd obviously been listening to every word. 'I've no intention of missing your wedding after all this, Fern Rycroft, even if I have to promise to drink no beer, eat no lamingtons and touch not a single oyster.'

The day dragged on after that.

Sam decided that he was staying in hospital for the

day, thank you very much, in case he had a relapse and Quinn agreed with such speed that Fern thought uncharitable thoughts about the account he was mentally preparing in his head.

'You could go home,' she told Sam, but he shook his head.

'I'm not risking it,' he said, folding his arms in a gesture of final decision. 'A man has to take care of his health—and in Dr Gallagher's hands I'm in very good hands.'

'I don't doubt it,' Fern agreed, casting a doubting glance at Quinn as he entered the room. There were dollar signs in his laughing eyes.

'He doesn't need to be here,' she told Quinn as they left together.

'Any suggestions how to shift him?' Quinn grinned. 'It doesn't bother me that he stays, Dr Rycroft. He's a paying customer and if I need the bed I'll move him somehow—even by enema if I have to.'

Fern laughed, but she was mortified all the same.

'Don't fret,' Quinn told her, seeing the doubt behind her smile. He touched her fleetingly on the cheek with a touch that felt as if it was charged with electricity. 'I'll take great care of your beloved. For you. . .'

He left her standing on the hospital steps, feeling more confused than she'd ever felt in her life.

Fern drove back to the farmhouse to find her uncle in deepest despair. He cheered up, though, when Fern told him of his wife's decision to have the operation and went off to the hospital to sit with her.

Fern was left facing the mess from the day before.

The mess suited her mood.

The lunch dishes were still unwashed from yesterday's ill-fated wedding lunch. The guests had gone straight from lunch to the church. 'We'll fix this mess later,' Maud had promised and here it was. . .later. There were still a couple of oysters, cold and congealed on plates around the room. Ugh!

Even after Fern had cleared the mess she cleaned on, polishing mirrors, searching for non-existent cobwebs...

Trying to block out Quinn Gallagher and his unwelcome offer...

She didn't feel the least bit tempted. She didn't...

Her uncle was being fed at the hospital. Fern made herself a sandwich for lunch and another for tea and then, toward dusk, she wandered down to the harbour.

It was as if she was in some sort of limbo—some waiting time—but she didn't know what she was waiting for.

It was a glorious night, a repeat performance of the night before. The island might be in the grip of drought, its grasses burned brown from a long hot summer, but in the dusk little of that was obvious. The moon shimmered into existence low on the horizon and slowly started to rise.

Fern dug her hands deep into the pockets of her jeans and walked slowly along the rows of boats representing Barega's fishing fleet. She knew each and every one of them. Normally they'd be out on a night like this—but most of the fishermen had been at the wedding...

Most had eaten Lizzy's oysters.

They'd still be feeling weak and washed out after last night's stomach upsets and the sea would have little appeal.

Fern walked slowly from boat to boat. They were as familiar as...as familiar as Sam.

She walked halfway down the jetty and then stopped dead as an unfamiliar sound smashed across the silence.

Fern turned, trying to figure out where the sound had come from.

There was another smash, the splintering of timber under something that sounded like an axe. Then a shout of horror echoed over the water from the end of the jetty and, as if driven by the shout, a diesel engine roared into life.

In the dim moonlight Fern saw a fishing boat swerve out from its moorings and head for the open sea. Fast!

It was Lizzy's boat. The fishing boat that Lizzy's father had operated before her. The *Dolphin*...

What on earth was the crash, though? Instinctively, Fern started to run toward the gap Lizzy's boat had left, her sneaker-clad feet moving swiftly on the jetty boards.

There was someone else there. The boat next to Lizzy's belonged to Alf Gunn. Alf was in his eighties and his boat was the old fisherman's only home. He slept below deck. Now he was standing on the jetty, rubbing his eyes as if waking from a bad dream.

'Alf, what is it?' Fern reached the old man and took his shoulders in her hands. The sense of urgency inside her was making her feel sick. She just knew...

'The girl...' Alf's voice was a disbelieving whisper. 'Lizzy... I heard the first smash and was up like a cork in a bottle of fizz, thinking it was vandals. It was Lizzy, miss. She's stove a ruddy great hole in her boat—in her lovely boat!—right below the Plimsoll line. And she's headed out to sea with water pouring in! Top speed...'

'Why...?'

They both knew why. The old man and the girl stared at each other in horror as they came to terms with what Lizzy had done.

'It's suicide, isn't it, Fern?' Alf said bleakly. 'After what she did yesterday...'

'I guess...' Fern's mind was racing at a hundred miles an hour. 'How big was the hole?'

'Big enough. Not so big that she'll go down in the harbour, though. Most of the hole was above water. It's only when the boat hits the ocean swell...'

Lizzy had thought this out well. If the boat went down in the harbour she wouldn't drown. She could swim like a fish. But if she got her boat out into the main ocean currents...and her boat sank.... There was no way Lizzy could change her mind after that.

'So we follow her,' Fern said frantically. 'Can we do it, Alf?'

'We don't have a choice,' Alf said grimly. 'Come on, girl!'

Alf was born on the boat and born to the sea. The same as Lizzy. It took such a one to follow Lizzy because the girl was moving with both desperation and skill.

From the mouth of the harbour a reef ran eastward in a foaming, jagged line. Lizzy's boat, lights cut, turned north—straight across the reef. If it hadn't been a moonlit night they wouldn't have seen her. As it was, Fern could hardly believe her eyes.

'She'll smash on the rocks,' Fern gasped.

'Not Lizzy,' Alf said grimly. 'Not that she'd mind if she did—but there's a gap, if you know the way. If she hits the reef she'll risk being washed up on the beach within minutes. It's my guess Lizzy doesn't want that to happen.'

'Do you know the way...?'

She didn't have to ask. Alf was already swinging his boat north and it was all Fern could do not to close her eyes in horror.

There was foam surging all around their boat and jagged rocks on either side. Surely this was impossible... In the dark...

It wasn't impossible. The boat lurched through the last breaking wave and surged on. Ahead of them was Lizzy's boat, sinking lower and lower in the water as she went.

'May it keep afloat another five minutes,' Alf said through gritted teeth, 'or she'll drift back onto the reef.'

His wish was granted. Lizzy's boat was gunned hard out to sea; it went on and on, its deck sinking to an impossible level...

Then it stopped dead. A swell must have caught it broadside and the huge mass of water below decks shifted.

The boat reared sideways and slowly, slowly, slipped under the water.

As it disappeared under the surface, a thin, forlorn figure raised her hands in the air and slipped beneath the waves with her boat.

CHAPTER SIX

'DEAR God!'

Alf had unconsciously gripped Fern's arm in—for Alf—an almost unheard-of gesture of emotional need. He'd throttled right back to dead still.

'The boat will suck her down,' Fern whispered.

'It's not big enough to pull her right down and hold her,' Alf said, as though thinking to himself. 'Too small a boat for huge suction. It'll put her down a way but she'll come up again—unless she's caught. . .'

'But. . .'

'She's aimed right for the middle of the slipstream.' Alf chewed his lip and then gunned his boat forward fast, slowing as they reached the point where Lizzy's boat had sunk. 'She's thought this out, all right.'

There was nothing to see. A vague turbulence swirled on the surface as though air was escaping from the cabin below but there was no Lizzy.

Alf cut his engine. He grabbed the lifebuoy on the side of the boat and tossed it overboard and then tossed a couple of life-jackets over, for good measure.

No one tried to swim to them.

There were no cries for help. Nothing.

There was dead silence apart from the slap of water against the wooden sides of Alf's boat.

Nothing at all to show that Lizzy had ever been here.

'She's gone. . .'

'She won't have drowned yet,' Alf said grimly. 'It's darned hard to make yourself drown if you're as strong a swimmer as Lizzy Hurst. The slipstream here runs straight out to sea and it's too strong to swim against. That's why she's come here, I reckon. Lizzy'll be carried out—and the only way we can stay within cooee of her is by letting ourselves be carried with her.'

'But, Alf. . .'

'Water pushes everything along at the same rate,' Alf muttered. He was talking more to himself than to Fern. 'See the lifebuoy and life-jackets I tossed over? They're still almost together. As soon as we start the engine we'll lose her. Drifting with her is our only hope. Her only hope.'

The old man cupped his hands around his mouth.

'Lizzy,' he yelled. 'We're here. Swim to us and stop being a damned fool. . .'

The old man stopped on a spurt of coughing.

'You yell,' he said grimly. 'My lungs aren't as strong as they used to be. I'm going below to see if I can find a torch.'

'Lizzy. . .'

Fern's yell drifted over the eerie silence like a hopeless dirge.

Ten seconds later Alf was back with his torch—a big flashlight with a powerful beam. He played it over the water while Fern yelled.

On Fern's tenth yell they both saw her, a frail floating figure that ducked under the surface as the spotlight hit her.

'Lizzy,' Fern screamed. 'Lizzy. . .'

'Go away. . .' The girl was within thirty yards of the boat, sobbing with despair. 'Go away. Let me drown. . .'

And she duck-dived again into the depths.

'We'll never get her,' Alf said morosely. 'Not if she don't want to be got. The water in this slipstream comes straight from the Antarctic, Fern. She'll get hypothermia and drown—that's if the sharks don't get her first.'

'Sharks. . .'

'Not many round here.' Alf moved the torch over the water again. Nothing. 'Water's too cold. But enough. . .'

'So. . .'

'If she wants to die, I don't see how we can stop her,' Alf said. 'Guess we just stay here in case she changes her mind. Maybe we ought to radio the local cop—not that he can do anything...'

Of course. The radio...

'Sam might be more use...'

'Beg pardon?' Alf queried but Fern was already clambering below, her thoughts converting to instant action. Fern had spent heaps of time on fishing boats as a teenager and knew how the radio worked. She needed Sam...

Sam thought he was ill. He wouldn't come.

He must.

Quinn Gallagher would get him here. The thought steadied her. If anyone could help, it was Quinn Gallagher...

There wasn't any logic in such a thought but Fern was beyond logic.

She wanted Quinn.

She had him.

Every building on the island was connected to marine radio and two minutes later Quinn picked up the radio in the hospital. One of the nurses had answered the relayed call and fetched him fast.

The fear in Fern's voice was enough to drive the slowest to speed.

'Fern...! What the...?'

Quinn's voice made Fern give a sob of relief. The fear took a tiny step back.

'Quinn, Quinn, is Sam still there?'

Quinn caught the tremor. There was a sharp intake of breath.

'What's wrong, Dr Rycroft?' Quinn Gallagher's voice was incisive—professional and competent. It cut across Fern's panic and steadied her further.

She was right. Quinn Gallagher was an emergency specialist. She needed him...

Swiftly she outlined what was happening, knowing that by transmitting on the distress frequency she'd have half the island listening.

It was best this way. There was no time for considering Lizzy's finer feelings now and the more islanders who knew what was happening the better chance Lizzy had.

'Sam's the only one who might...might make her respond,' Fern told Quinn as she faltered to a halt. 'If he were here and calling—instead of me. She might come if it was Sam who wanted her.'

'I'll get him out there if I have to get four strong men to carry him,' Quinn promised grimly. 'Fast. Keep the line open, Fern. Is there any fisherman listening who can take Sam Hubert out to sea...?'

The line crackled with offers.

Most islanders left their radios permanently on by their kitchen tables, tuned low to the distress frequency—just in case. They were a long way from the mainland and the islanders looked after their own. Clearly now the whole island had been listening to the story, aghast.

'OK, Dr Rycroft,' Quinn said softly as the offers faded. 'We have everything we need to move fast. Hang in there, Fern. We're on our way.'

They didn't come in one boat. The boat bringing Sam headed a small flotilla.

Ten minutes after the call Barega's fishing fleet surged out of the harbour in a display of strength that would have made the Armada think twice before invading the island. Their lights twinkled on an already moonlit ocean and if it hadn't been so deadly serious Fern could have been captivated by their beauty.

She hardly noticed.

Neither she nor Alf had seen Lizzy now for fifteen minutes.

Lizzy must still be somewhere near them, though. The life-jackets and buoy were still floating by the boat. The current was too strong to swim against. All they had to do was drift on and hope that somewhere close Lizzy was drifting too.

Alf had his lights on full. The fishing fleet couldn't

miss them, although the currents had now carried them almost two miles out to sea.

They just had to wait...

And wait...

The fleet stopped three hundred yards from Alf's boat. The fishermen would know that for twenty boats to churn round searching for a girl who didn't want to be found would probably succeed in cutting her to ribbons on someone's propeller.

The leading boat edged forward, spotlights spanning out over the water, and Fern recognised a team of Barega's most able fishermen on the deck of the *Wave Dancer*.

Their boat was too high, though. The *Wave Dancer* was six times as big as Alf's *Jeanie*. It was too far from the surface for anyone to reach down to Lizzy—if she swam to the side.

The fishermen knew it. The men were already launching a rubber dinghy from the side. It dropped fast to the water's surface with two men on board.

Sam...

And Quinn...

What on earth was Quinn doing here? Surely he should be with Maud...

Maybe he'd needed to carry out his threat—and carry Sam bodily down to the boat...

If Maud had another cardiac arrest...

She couldn't think of her aunt now. Fern's eyes turned back to the water, searching uselessly. Where on earth was Lizzy? Had she slipped away from them?

She'd been in the water for over half an hour.

Only Alf's boat and the little dinghy were left floating together in the slipstream now. *Wave Dancer* had backed off about three hundred yards as soon as the dinghy was launched but its vast spotlights still lit the surface of the water like day.

In the background the fishing fleet waited.

It seemed as if the whole world waited.

Lizzy Hurst might be slightly crazy but she was

one of the island's own and every man and woman in this fleet wanted only one thing. They wanted their Lizzy back.

Fern had never felt so much part of the island. She looked across at the massed lights and felt her throat thicken. To be part of this...

There were worse things than to be part of this...

She wasn't an islander. She wasn't!

'Lizzy...'

Sam's booming voice across the water made her wince.

Every boat had cut its engine and the silence was intense. Sam had a carrying lawyer's voice at the best of times and in his hand he now held a megaphone.

With the megaphone, Sam's voice was enough to make anyone respond. That, or face the consequences...

'Lizzy!'

To Fern's amazement she heard Sam's normally carefully modulated, professional voice crack with emotion.

Sam? Emotional? Not the Sam Fern knew.

There was no doubting the fear in Sam's voice now.

'Lizzy, you have to come back,' he shouted. 'This is crazy, girl. I can't let you drown...because of me...'

Then a soft cry sounded out over the water and Fern's breath went out in a rush.

'Let me go.'

Lizzy's sad, defeated voice drifted over the ocean like an echo and Fern's fingers clenched into her palms. 'I want to die...' the voice whispered. 'You love her...'

So Lizzy was still alive.

Sam's body stiffened perceptibly. He twisted where he sat in the dinghy so that he was facing where the voice had come from.

'Hell, Liz...' Sam's voice broke into the megaphone but started again at doubled strength, sure now that he was being heard. 'Hell, Lizzy, you'd make an awful lawyer's wife!'

This was a crazy, crazy conversation.

'Go away. . .'

Then, to her horror, Fern saw Sam stand up in the rubber dinghy. He swayed precariously.

Unlike most of the islanders, Sam had not a sea leg to stand on. Quinn, sitting facing him, saw the danger and hauled him down hard.

It seemed that Quinn at least was keeping his head.

'Lizzy, please. . .' Sam pleaded.

'I won't make any wife at all. . .' The echo drifted around them. 'I'm drowning. . .'

'No!'

Sam's voice was rising to a howl of outrage as if something deep inside him had suddenly snapped. The big man shoved against Quinn's restraining hand and then, before Quinn could stop him, the lawyer launched himself out into the water.

No graceful dive here. Sam made a splash like a very large rock, going down.

'Sam. . .'

It was Lizzy's voice again. She'd seen. There was terror in her voice for the first time. She hadn't been afraid for herself. . .but for her love. . .

'Shark!'

The word boomed out from behind them and Fern swung round. The lights of the *Wave Dancer* had been playing over the water in all directions, trying to find Lizzy. Now. . . Now one beam played on a black fin, moving fast.

'Sam. . .' Fern heard herself screaming, her voice adding to the scream of the girl in the water. 'Lizzy. . .'

Alf was back at the tiller, his motor spluttering into frantic life and shattering the silence. They couldn't see Lizzy but they could see Sam. He was twenty yards from the dinghy, swimming with clumsy, heavy-handed strokes.

'Don't swim,' Fern screamed. It was Sam's thrashing that would attract the shark—though it would have been lured first by the fishing boats. The boats often cleaned their kill after their catch and the sharks knew that the boats meant an easy feed.

'No... Sam...!' The voice was Lizzy's again, faint against the roar of Alf's engine. It was a scream of frantic fear and, thirty yards from Sam, Fern saw Lizzy start to swim desperately toward her love.

'Take over, Fern. Get in as close as you can...' Alf hauled Fern in to the tiller. 'Move, girl.'

Now that Alf could see both people in the water there was no danger of hitting them with the propeller—and if there was a choice of propeller or shark, Fern would choose a propeller any time. At least a propeller travelled in a straight line. A swimmer had a chance to duck. It didn't swerve in any direction, with its mouth open and teeth razor sharp...

Fern moved without question as Alf clambered to the bow, grabbing something from a niche above the scuppers on the way. This was his domain. As Fern expected a nurse in Casualty to jump to orders, here Fern was subordinate.

There was a motor on the dinghy. Quinn had it started already and the dinghy was starting to move. He'd reach Lizzy and Sam before Alf's boat could and with the dinghy's increased manoeuvrability...

A scream smashed out over the water, and it was a scream of agony.

Sam...

'No!' Lizzy's voice was a rising well of despair. 'Sam...'

Where the girl found the strength after so long in the water Fern couldn't tell, but Lizzy swam to Sam like a woman possessed. Lizzy reached him before either fishing boat or dinghy, grabbing the big man and pulling him over to lie in her arms.

The shark had already struck.

Sam lay motionless, hanging heavy with shock against Lizzy's slight body.

From somewhere below an ugly stain drifted to the surface, red in the spotlight's beams.

And the dark fin was moving in again.

Alf's shout from the bow made Fern blink. 'Hard back on the throttle. Now, girl!'

Fern shoved back hard, and the noise died as the motor stalled...

Then another took its place.

It seemed like the world exploded.

The long thin object Alf had grabbed from above the scuppers was a gun. And Alf had just used it...

The shotgun looked like some crazy, theatrical blunderbuss. It looked useless...a joke...

Fern stared from the gun down to the water. The boat was drifting broadside to the swell, letting Fern see those in the water.

The gun had done what Alf intended.

The shark was blasted beyond belief. The water was deep crimson with gore and Quinn's dinghy had almost reached the pair in the water.

Alf's action had bought them only seconds of safety.

They wouldn't be safe now, even in the dinghy.

With so much blood, every shark worthy of the name would be here in minutes. They'd rip apart what was left of their companion and in a feeding frenzy nothing would survive. A rubber dinghy was little protection against such a frenzy...

Apart from the dinghy, Alf's boat was the lowest and the nearest. Fern already had the motor started again and in gear, and Alf was leaning over the side with the grappling hook.

'Port, girl... A bit more...'

She couldn't see now. From the back of the boat where Fern held the tiller she was steering blind. Only Alf on the bow had any idea.

'Slow... Slow...Cut the motor!'

Once again she cut the motor.

'Come up here, girl...Fern, get here...'

Alf had the dinghy secure against the side of his boat

with the grappling iron and in the dinghy Quinn had Lizzy under her arms, trying to haul her out of the water.

It was some feat as Lizzy was holding on to Sam for dear life.

The whole dinghy was threatening to capsize. The side of the dinghy where Quinn held Lizzy was dipping almost underwater.

'Hold this, Fern.' Alf shoved the grappling iron into Fern's hands.

For a man in his eighties, Alf was moving lightning fast. A man a quarter of his age couldn't have moved with this speed. As Fern took the grappling hook he disappeared and was back in seconds with rope to secure the rubber craft to the side of the fishing boat.

From nearby the rest of the fleet watched helplessly. There was no time to launch another boat...and their fishing boats were too high...

Then Alf was back. Almost before he'd secured the dinghy, Quinn had assessed what was happening. With the dinghy safe from sinking he could act.

'OK, Lizzy,' Quinn ordered harshly and his words were tight with strain from hauling the two sodden figures. His voice was still strong enough, though, to cut into Lizzy's exhaustion. 'You have to help me. Pull Sam forward and then hang on to the dinghy rope. Now!'

The girl in the water cast a hopeless look back up at Quinn but something in Quinn's authoritative tone must have got through. She was so exhausted now that the only thing possible was to follow orders.

Fern held her breath. Without Lizzy's assistance Quinn could do nothing and the dinghy wasn't big enough to take anyone else's weight. Neither she nor Alf could help. But if Lizzy held on herself... If she forgot she was intent on suicide...

She had forgotten. With a jagging effort Lizzy hauled Sam further forward and Quinn grabbed him by the collar. Then Lizzy's hands caught the handhold on the dinghy's side.

'Can you pull Lizzy up?' Quinn demanded of the two in the boat.

'Sure thing, Doc,' Alf said as though he were agreeing to pass the salt. 'Hang on to me, Fern, girl.'

The old man quickly leaned over to the side of the dinghy. Fern grabbed him by the belt as Alf caught Lizzy by the hand and pulled.

He'd never have done it alone.

As soon as she was sure that Alf had his balance, Fern let him go and reached down to grab Lizzy's other hand. The girl came on board in a sodden, slithery rush.

Fern and Alf hardly had time to see her crumple to the deck. They were back, leaning over to grab Sam from Quinn's clasp and haul him aboard.

Sam came with more than sea water. A gush of blood followed him on board. Alf was still helping Quinn over the side as Fern started frantically trying to staunch the flow.

It wasn't as bad as it could have been.

He wasn't dead.

There was a massive wound on Sam's side. The shark's teeth had sliced into his right loin, tearing away skin, muscle and. . .

And what else, Fern hated to think. Heaven knew what damage had been done under the bleeding but for now the bleeding was the only thing that Fern could worry about. With a wound this size he'd be dead in minutes.

So all Fern had to do was stop the bleeding.

All. . .

The pressure points. . .Where were the pressure points here? For heaven's sake, what was she dealing with?

'OK, Sam,' she managed to say in a voice that was almost even. 'You're safe now. . .'

Sam gave an agonised grunt; his head rolled to one side and he slid into unconsciousness.

May he stay that way until they had some morphine!

Frantically Fran tried to assess the wound, feeling in the dim light the extent of the torn flesh and where the bulk of the bleeding was coming from. No pressure point would stop abdominal bleeding. The only thing that might help was pressure on the wound itself.

Fern had looped her cotton windcheater round her waist when she had come out for her walk—hours ago, it seemed now.

There was sacking on the deck—but it stank of rotten fish and the consequences of using that were horrible to contemplate. The windcheater would have to do.

Swiftly Fern folded it into a heavy pad. Then her hands went straight to Sam's loin, shoving in hard.

Harder. . .

The gushing blood slowed to an ooze. . .

On the deck beside her, Lizzy was whimpering with shock and exhaustion. She'd be suffering from hypothermia, Fern thought grimly, but there was no time for Lizzy now. . .

Heavens, she couldn't cope with this by herself.

Dear God. . .

'What's the damage?'

Quinn's voice cut her panic dead. Unnoticed by Fern, Alf had helped haul Quinn aboard from the dinghy. Now Quinn knelt beside her, eyes cool and appraising.

There was no panic here.

'We need blankets, Alf,' Quinn said brusquely, as he took in what Fern was doing. His eyes moved momentarily to Lizzy, noting her absolute exhaustion. 'And, Alf, strip the girl, wrap her and get her below. Get her warm fast. How bad is it here, Dr Rycroft?'

From his tone they might have been back in the casualty department of a major hospital, with all its resources at their disposal. The horror of the night receded a little as professionalism took over.

Sam—this man lying here bleeding to death on the deck—might be the man she intended to marry but with Quinn's harsh approach Fern could switch back into clinical efficiency. Sam became a patient.

A patient with life-threatening injuries.

'There's flesh ripped right out from the side of his abdomen. I can't see——but his bowel may be involved, at the very least. Heaven knows what else. The wound's maybe eight inches across...'

'Right. Hold on there while I fix his position.'

Quinn glanced round fast. Beside them was a piece of planking that Alf used to wheel crates of fish from deck to jetty.

It was perfect.

Quinn hauled the planking across beside Sam. The lawyer was still heavily unconscious, his skin pale, cold and clammy. He'd die of shock and blood loss, Fern thought desperately.

'We need to get him back to the island,' she whispered. 'It's his only hope. We need saline... plasma...morphine...'

'There's saline and morphine in my bag. It's on the other boat. I yelled at them to bring it over while I was still on the dinghy.' Quinn was working as he talked, tucking the planking as far under Sam as it would go without lifting Sam's body. He looked at Fern's gory hands, noting the slowing bleeding. 'Hold tight. I'm moving the top half...'

With a swift tug he shifted Sam's head and chest onto the boards. Without pausing for breath he was down at Sam's thighs, lifting the rest of Sam's body across without disturbing what Fern had achieved.

Then to Sam's feet...

There were folded craypots lying nearby. Quinn lifted the planking with an audible grunt of effort and shoved a couple of folded craypots underneath at foot level. Sam's body was now lying with head down and the lower part of his body elevated.

It'd help a bit.

Enough?

Alf emerged from the cabin. He'd taken an unprotesting Lizzy below, half carrying her, and he must have undressed and wrapped her with lightning speed. For a fleeting moment it crossed Fern's mind to wonder just how many young women this crusty old bachelor had been asked to undress in his time but the thought wasn't enough to bring a smile to her lips. Not now...

Alf's arms were loaded with blankets.

'Lizzy's crook,' he said grimly. 'I undressed her like you'd undress a rag doll. I've put her in my bunk with the electric blanket up full.'

'Electric blanket?' Quinn was ripping off Sam's sodden shirt and already tucking Alf's offering of thick wool around him. It was vital that they get Sam warm as well—but they couldn't shift him below. The less movement the better with a wound like this. 'How the heck...?'

'Big batteries.' Alf grimaced. 'A man's gotta have some comfort. What can I do now, Doc?'

'Get my bag, if you can,' Quinn told him. 'It's on the *Wave Dancer*.'

The *Wave Dancer*—the huge boat that had brought out Quinn and Sam—was almost alongside. The crews of the boats must be frantic, Fern realised. They wouldn't have a clue what was happening.

Then Alf had the motor running again. It was foolhardy for two boats to be alongside when one was without a motor—dangerous at the best of times.

The men knew what they were doing, though. Fern and Quinn could stick to their medicine. If there was one thing the fishermen of Barega were good at, it was coping with the sea.

The boats were manoeuvred as though they were on a lake at midday instead of an ocean swell after dark. In two minutes there were more men clambering onto the deck of Alf's boat and Quinn's precious bag was with them.

Morphine... Saline... Everything they needed to try to keep Sam alive...

Everything except luck...

He'd need that, Fern thought grimly, feeling Sam's cold and clammy skin. Luck, luck and more luck...

There was a sharp exclamation of horror from the bow of the boat and Fern glanced up in time to see the men drag aboard what was left of the dinghy.

Fern's fear of a shark feeding frenzy had been realised. The dinghy was torn to ribbons.

Sam had been lucky already.

And at least Sam had Quinn Gallagher, Fern thought with gratitude, as Quinn set up a saline drip with a speed she'd never seen before.

If ever there was a man to have around in an emergency it was this man.

If ever there was a man to have around...

Over the next few hours Sam hovered between life and death but by three in the morning Quinn's skill had loaded the dice in favour of life.

By three in the morning Fern was so exhausted that she was almost past caring.

They'd brought Sam back to Theatre and spent four gruelling hours trying to stem the bleeding and do emergency repairs.

If Quinn hadn't been a skilled surgeon they wouldn't have had a hope. The wound was horrendous.

At least the kidneys were clear. Their first task as they reached the hospital was to insert a catheter and watch for blood. The clear urine was the first piece of good news they'd had all night.

There was more.

It was just as well that Sam's blood group was O positive—if he'd had a rare blood type the task of cross-matching enough blood with the island's limited supplies would have been a nightmare.

With unit after unit of blood dripping into his veins to make up for the massive blood loss, Quinn assessed the wound and decided that his only choice was a full laparotomy. They didn't have a clue what damage there was.

If there was liver damage...

It didn't bear thinking of.

Quinn worked fast but thoroughly, cleaning and debriding the wound as he found and tied off the mass of tiny torn blood vessels that made the wound bleed so freely.

Fern gave the anaesthetic—a job that required her full attention with a patient who was so badly shocked—and could only marvel at the skills Quinn showed.

This man had been trained with the best. He was cool, swift and skilled but he was no textbook surgeon. This sort of surgery—repair of a wound so horribly different—took courage and intelligence, both of which Quinn seemed to have in abundance.

Barega was indeed blessed to have him here.

The bowel had been ripped and a small section completely torn out. Such a wound would have left Fern helpless with horror but Quinn didn't falter. He hardly talked during the reanastomosis—the joining of the torn ends of the bowel—or as he performed a meticulous peritoneal lavage, carefully washing out the abdominal cavity. Slipshod work here would cost Sam his life.

This was no slipshod work.

The fingers doing the surgical procedures were skilled and sure and Fern knew that Sam wouldn't be in any better hands if he'd been in Sydney.

The two island nurses stayed in Theatre and it took the four of them, working flat out, to give Sam a chance of life. This job in a major teaching hospital would have warranted a team of seven or eight. Here they had to make do with what they had.

Fern could only marvel as she watched Quinn sew the abdomen closed. There was still a massive defect— the dressing had to be applied over an area with no skin—but Sam now had a chance.

Finally, Quinn had done all he could. Fern adjusted intravenous antibiotics to maximum dosage and reversed the anaesthetic as the last dressing was put in place.

Quinn's work had been little short of brilliant. It was now up to Sam...

When Quinn wearily pushed his mask from his face, it was more than he who sighed with relief. The nurses pushed the trolley away with their shoulders sagging in exhaustion. Neither nurse had been in such an intense surgical situation since their training hospital—and even then Fern doubted that they'd been under such pressure.

'That was... That was magnificent...' Fern told Quinn as she walked unsteadily over to the sink. She hauled her own mask from her face with a feeling of unreality.

'It wasn't too bad a job you did yourself, Dr Rycroft,' Quinn told her and Fern flashed him a look of astonishment.

'You don't even sound exhausted.'

'I guess I am,' he admitted, 'but I've gone onto automatic pilot.'

'Some automatic pilot. It's saved Sam's life...'

'I just hope that's right. It'll be days before we know for sure. His chances of infection are still high. You realise he'll have to go to Sydney? It's a rough job I've done tonight. Cosmetic stuff will have to be done by the plastic guys.'

'As long as he lives...'

'As you say.'

Fern closed her eyes, exhaustion sweeping over her in waves. The urgent needs past, she felt just plain sick.

Quinn stepped behind her and untied the ribbons of her surgical gown. He flicked his gloves into the waste bin and then put his hands on her waist.

'You're all done, Dr Rycroft,' he said gently. He pulled her back to lean against him and she was too tired to care...

Not true.

She was too tired to resist.

'Bed, I think, Dr Rycroft.' Quinn's head dropped and he planted a light kiss on her hair.

'I. . .I think so. . .'

'You realise you lost a fiancé tonight?'

Quinn's voice was coming from a very long way away. Fern leaned back against his chest and let his words drift. They didn't make an awful lot of sense.

What had he said?

'Sam's going to live,' she said unsteadily. 'I know he is.'

'Not with you, he's not.'

'Why. . .?'

She had to force herself to ask the question. What Quinn was saying didn't seem to matter. What mattered was the feel of his arms around her, the feeling that here—against this man's body—she was secure against all peril.

The nightmare of the night was just that—a nightmare. It couldn't touch her now. She was with Quinn.

She was home.

You don't have a home, remember, Fern? a tiny voice whispered into the back of her head. That voice had been a shout since the night her parents died. Now the shout was fading almost to oblivion.

'Your Sam nearly went crazy when we told him what Lizzy was doing—that she was drowning,' Quinn said gently across her thoughts. His arms didn't slacken for a moment. She was enfolded in a cocoon of compassion as he spoke.

'I have to admit I thought the man incapable of passion. When I told him Lizzy would drown without him, though, he was out of his bed in seconds. He insisted point-blank I go with him; his theory was that I was a better trained doctor than you, and his Lizzy—*his* Lizzy—was going to have the best.

'I still had Maud to consider and you were already out with Lizzy so I refused and I thought Sam would kill me. So it wasn't me threatening to pick up Sam and take him out to sea—it was the other way round!'

'Sam...' Fern said faintly.

'Sam.'

Quinn's arms tightened even further. Surely this wasn't a professional approach at comfort by one imparting bad news...

Surely this was something more.

'Jess came back from her rounds just then—fortunately,' Quinn told her. 'She can do cardio-pulmonary resuscitation and can operate the defibrillator if necessary and she offered to stay with Maud before Sam did me physical violence. But it was a close thing.'

'Sam...Sam and Lizzy have always been friends,' Fern whispered. 'Sam and Lizzy and me.'

'Well, I think you have to face it.' Quinn swung Fern round in a gentle but firm movement so that her weary, shadowed face was looking up at him. 'Fern, I think tonight the "me" was taken out of the equation.'

'You don't know...'

'I do know,' he told her, his eyes never leaving her face. Quinn's hands were on her shoulders and without their support she would have toppled. 'I thought your Sam was incapable of passion and I was right. He was. Your Sam is. Lizzy's Sam, though...'

'I don't want to hear this...'

There was a long silence. The theatre clock ticked above their heads and that was the only sound there was.

'You have to hear it, Fern,' Quinn said softly at last. 'I just wish to blazes I could make you stop looking like that...'

'Like...'

'Like a woman Sam's crazy to abandon... Like a woman I could...'

He didn't finish. He couldn't. What was growing between them was too strong for words.

Fern didn't have to wonder this time whether she raised her lips in invitation to be kissed. She knew she did.

It was no act of flirtation or seduction, though. It

was two magnetic poles finding their home. The force pulling them together was something that Fern had never felt in her life before.

She only knew it felt right.

At that moment they had no separate will—only their mutual need—only their mutual acceptance of what was right.

They stayed, locked together, for what could have been hours. Fern didn't know. The clock ticked above them and Quinn's lips stayed on hers. His hands held her waist to his body and there was no other movement.

There was no need for further movement.

This wasn't passionate love-making. It was a process of healing—of bringing together two parts of a separate whole.

The aching void that had been in Fern since the night her family was killed was closing, filling, as though the link between herself and Quinn was feeding her something as essential as the plasma they had placed in Sam's veins. This wasn't blood, though. It was a nectar so sweet that it made her want to cry.

But she couldn't cry when she was here.

She couldn't cry when she was being kissed by someone like Quinn.

He was still wearing his bloodstained surgical gown and the jeans Fern had on were even more gory than his surgical greens. It didn't matter. The time for dissembling was over.

There was only Quinn...

She opened her lips to him and her aching heart felt as though it opened at the same time, allowing the sweetness of love to flow through...

His hands came up under her blouse, cupping her breasts with fingers that were exquisitely gentle. It was as if he was touching the most precious thing this world had to offer, Fern thought, and knew that her thought was truth.

What was flowering between them was a gift—a gift so precious that none could deny it.

Certainly not Fern.

Her body arched against him and she heard herself give a soft moan of sheer ecstasy.

He broke away then, holding her at arm's length, her bloodstained blouse falling back into position. His eyes were dark and demanding, claiming his own.

'This is right,' he said, and his voice was thick with suppressed passion. 'Hell, Fern, you can't marry Sam after this. You know you can't.'

'I know. . .' Her voice trailed to a whisper.

'You belong with me.' His hands gripped more tightly, possessive and urgent. 'You feel it too, don't you, Fern? Whoever else has claims—on either of us— we're one, Fern Rycroft. I felt it the moment I set eyes on you—and we're wasting time by denying it. . .'

'S-Sam. . .' Fern whispered. 'I have to speak to Sam. . .' Her tired mind was going round and round in circles. She only wanted to be with this man—with Quinn, with her heart—and yet she was still engaged to Sam. She shouldn't be here, letting Quinn make love to her, when in the next room her fiancé was fighting for his life.

'You have to speak to Sam,' Quinn agreed, pulling her tight to him again. 'And I. . .I have organising of my own to do. But that's all it is, my lovely Fern. Reorganising our lives so we can be in our rightful place. Together.'

'I don't know,' Fern whispered. Her heart was thumping with fear, doubt and passion all at the one time. 'Maybe. . .'

'There's no "maybe" about it, Fern Rycroft,' Quinn growled thickly into her hair. He tilted her chin again so she was looking wonderingly up at him. 'There's only us.'

'Are you still here?'

A woman's light voice, calling from the doorway around the partition from the sink, was the first thing that intruded from the outside world.

Heaven knew how long the voice had been calling. The kiss was deep enough to blot out all but the loudest of alarms.

Quinn swore unsteadily as the lingering kiss finally ceased and they pulled apart. He didn't release Fern entirely, though—just pulled her round to stand beside him, his arm still encircling her waist.

It seemed almost a gesture of propriety, of possessiveness, though Fern still felt that she'd topple over without his supporting arm. The combination of weariness, shock, relief and. . .and the nearness of Quinn. . . was making her dizzy.

It was Jessie.

The young vet peered anxiously around the partition and smiled with relief when she saw them.

'Here you are. I was starting to think Quinn must have driven you home, Fern, and I rang your uncle hours ago to tell him we'd give you a bed here.'

'C-can you?' The feeling of unreality was deepening, if anything.

'Of course we can.' Jessie smiled from Quinn to Fern, seemingly oblivious to the position of Quinn's arm and the burning colour of Fern's cheeks. 'Lizzy's in the ward with your aunt, though, so you can't stay there. We've packed Lizzy with hot-water bottles and sedated her. Her temp's back up to normal. She was still restless until you finished in Theatre and one of the nurses came in to tell her Sam would most likely live. Now she's sleeping like a baby.'

'You. . .you sedated her?'

'Needs must,' Jessie grinned. 'It's not so different from sedating a horse.' Then, at Fern's look, she laughed and relented. 'OK, Quinn gave me instructions before he went to Theatre—while you were prepping Sam.'

'I. . .I see. . .'

'I don't think you see very much at all,' Jessie corrected her kindly. 'Fern, you look as exhausted as Lizzy. Bring her down to bed, Quinn. . .'

'But...'

'I have a huge bedroom and two beds,' Jessie assured her. 'And I take my parrot up to the kitchen at night—so there's no need to worry about anything but my snoring. Quinn, you're not going to bed yet?'

'Not yet. Not until Sam's fully recovered from the anaesthetic and settled into natural sleep. It could be a couple of hours.'

'Then Fern and I had better sleep so that at least someone's functioning in the morning.' Jessie's kindly eyes assessed Fern's face. 'Can you walk, Fern, or does Quinn have to carry you?'

'I can...'

She couldn't.

Fern didn't finish her sentence. Quinn had already swung her up in his arms and was heading for the door, squeezing all the protest out of her.

'For a very clever vet, you ask some very silly questions, Jess,' he smiled back at the vet, but the tenderness on his smile was all for Fern. 'My lady has her own method of transport.'

CHAPTER SEVEN

FERN slept the sleep of the dead.

When finally she woke the sun was pouring in over her bedcovers and Jessie was walking towards the bed carrying a tray.

'Bacon on toast and coffee,' she smiled. 'Hungry?'

'Y-yes.' Fern rubbed her eyes.

Then she rubbed them again. Jessie seemed to have grown a new breast in the night.

As she stared, the middle breast wriggled.

'OK, you,' Jessie said placidly, cradling the extra breast in the cup of her palm. 'I know it's time for another feed.'

She grinned down at Fern's look of astonishment.

'I've won another baby in the night,' she said. 'A tiny wombat. One of the local farmers found it in his back paddock when he went to check on a calving. I'm not sure of its chances—it seems badly shocked—but this way at least it has a hope. My movement, warmth and heartbeat are the closest approximation I can get to his mum.'

'I...see...'

This place was a madhouse. Hospital, home, veterinary clinic, orphanage...

They were so busy. It was great of Jessie to bring her breakfast. Fern glanced at the bedside clock.

And glanced again.

Eleven o'clock!

It couldn't be.

'It sure is,' Jessie smiled, seeing Fern's look of astonishment. 'I thought if you didn't have this now you'd be running breakfast into lunch. Besides...' she sat down on the bed in comfortable companionship, still stroking her wriggling extra breast '...the air ambulance is due in half an hour to take Sam to the mainland and we thought you'd want to say goodbye.'

'Oh... Of course...' Fern took the mug of coffee with gratitude. She sipped and sipped again and her crazy world finally tilted back to the right way up. 'How is...how is Sam?'

'His obs are good so far,' Jessie told her. 'Quinn has the morphine so topped up he's hardly conscious—but his blood pressure's holding and Quinn's happy with his electrolytes and his haemoglobin level. Things are looking good.'

'And Lizzy...?'

Jessie cast her a sideways look. 'She's packing.'

'Packing!'

'That's what I said. Quinn told her an hour ago that Sam was being taken to Sydney for plastic surgery and she flew out of bed and headed home. She said she'd be back with a suitcase and if we let Sam go without her she'd murder the lot of us.'

'Oh...'

'It seems Sam Hubert has some decisions to make,' Jessie said gently, her eyes warm with sympathy, but Fern shook her head.

'No,' she whispered. 'I don't think he has.'

Her clothes from the night before were disgusting. Jessie had lent Fern a nightgown to sleep in and now she offered a light skirt and blouse.

'It's lucky we're almost the same size,' Jessie smiled, and Fern shook her head.

'Your blouse hangs loose.' Fern grimaced and gave the top button of the skirt up as a lost cause. 'You're too darned thin.'

'Yeah, well, I haven't always been this thin. There are silver linings to every dark cloud,' Jess said enigmatically.

Once again Fern looked at the dark shadows around Jessie's eyes and wondered.

It was none of her business but the warmth she was

feeling towards Jessie made her wish very much that Jessie, one day, would tell her what was causing the shadows. Fern had the feeling that in Jessie there could be a friend.

Quinn met them as they emerged into the corridor.

His eyes lit at the sight of Fern. Even for a man trained to cope with sleep deprivation there was weariness around Quinn's eyes this morning.

Fern's heart stirred at the sight of it. It was all she could do not to put her hand up to smooth away the lines of fatigue.

'You should be in bed, Dr Gallagher,' she said gently. 'I can take over now.'

He smiled down at her, his smile a caress, and the wrenching sensation in her heart turned to something else entirely. Something like jelly.

'Let's get rid of your Sam and then we'll think about bed.' His smile deepened and Fern gasped. There was no mistaking the gleam of wickedness in those eyes.

'Dr Gallagher...' she whispered unsteadily.

'Dr Rycroft!' His voice was a parrot-like imitation of her shocked tone. He motioned to the door. 'You'll be wanting to see Sam before he goes. He's awake— just—and he has the ward to himself. We let Frank go home this morning. He was whinging that a man couldn't get any sleep in a place like this and I reckon if Frank's well enough to whinge he's well enough to go home. So you have privacy.'

'Th-thank you.' Fern walked uncertainly forward.

Quinn opened Sam's door for her and let her pass.

'Go and bid your love goodbye, Fern,' he said softly. 'Though I don't think that's really right, is it, Dr Rycroft? Go in and say goodbye to your friend.'

Sam was drifting in and out of sleep.

The nursing sister was sitting by the bed. Geraldine looked up and smiled as Fern walked in and then rose and left.

It was as though Quinn had given her orders to leave Sam and Fern alone.

'Call me when you leave him,' the nurse whispered, 'and I'll come back.'

Fern nodded.

She took the seat the nurse had just vacated, leaned over and touched Sam's hand.

Sam's eyes flicked open.

'Fern...'

'I'm here,' she whispered. 'You're OK. The plane will be here soon to take you to Sydney—the plastic surgeons there can do a better cosmetic job than we can. You'll need a skin graft to replace some of your torn skin.'

'Where's Lizzy...?'

Fern took a deep breath. 'She's gone home to pack. She says she's coming with you.'

Sam's eyes widened at that. 'Lizzy... She wouldn't do that...Would she? Leave the island?'

'She won't let you go alone.' Fern took Sam's big hand in hers. 'Lizzy loves you, Sam. I don't know what you're going to do about it but there it is...'

Sam took a deep breath. He stirred, winced and closed his eyes. 'I'm going to marry her,' he said, and his voice, despite his injuries, was firm.

Silence. The room was warmed with the morning sun still streaming in the windows. Sam's words drifted round and round like the end of a story.

A 'happy ever after' ending...

Strange. This conversation should be uncomfortable, at the very least. Sam was Fern's fiancé and here he was, announcing that he'd changed his mind. Announcing that he'd marry another...

Fern had never felt uncomfortable with Sam, though.

He was her friend.

Not her love.

She only had room in her heart for one...

'Don't let Lizzy blackmail you into it,' she teased lightly and Sam gripped her hand, opened his eyes and met her look.

'I won't let her do that. Fern, I've been thinking...'

'What have you been thinking?'

'Well. . .' Sam's voice died away as if gathering strength but his lawyer's ability to argue a case won the day.

'You and me. . .We're fond of each other. Right?'

'Right.'

'But you'd never poison people on my behalf. . .or try to drown yourself. . .'

Fern's lips twitched. 'No,' she agreed, her voice a trifle unsteady. 'I'd never do that.'

'I think I want that.'

Fern swallowed. She nodded wisely and fought for the right words. 'You don't. . .you don't think you might find poisoning and drowning just. . .just a trifle unsettling?'

Despite her fight for control, Sam heard the laughter bubble through Fern's words and the lawyer managed a smile in response.

'Hell, Fern, I wouldn't be the least bit surprised if I do,' he whispered. 'But. . .but last night I nearly lost here. And I realised. . .I realised what I was losing. . .'

He broke off.

The door had opened behind them. There was a tiny whimper of sound and Sam's gaze shifted to see who had just entered.

It was Lizzy. His love. . .

'Lizzy, love. . .' Sam whispered, acknowledging finally what Lizzy had always known, and Fern was forgotten.

Lizzy must have heard every word.

She'd come in looking defiant but now. . .now every trace of defiance on the girl's face crumpled to nothing. With a sob the girl ran across the room and buried her face on the coverlet.

'Oh, Sam. . . Oh, Sam. . .'

'Don't cry, Liz,' Sam whispered, his hand releasing Fern to stroke Lizzy's hair. 'It'll be right. I guess we have to sort things out after this—so we can stay together. I can come back to the island and practise law. Somehow...somehow being a big-shot city lawyer doesn't seem such a good deal—after last night.'

'I'll live in the city with you,' Lizzy sobbed. 'I was crazy to say I wouldn't. You don't have to come home because of me.'

'We'll see,' Sam whispered.

Fern smiled again. She could see what was in Sam's mind. The havoc Lizzy Hurst could wreak in the city could be horrendous. Poisoning a whole island of people could be cast into insignificance.

'I'll leave you, then,' she said, and neither of them heard.

She had no place here—between lovers.

'Thank you, Fern,' Sam whispered, as he finally realised she was leaving, but he had eyes only for his Lizzy.

'So, how does it feel to be a jilted bride?'

Quinn was waiting for Fern in the corridor, his words sympathetic but his eyes still dangerous.

Lizzy had left the door open.

Quinn must have heard enough.

Fern smiled right back. Right at this minute being jilted didn't seem all that bad. It was somehow as if a rather large weight had been lifted from her shoulders.

Her world was very much the right way up this morning.

With Quinn smiling at her like that, miracles were possible.

Miracles were probable.

She laughed up into his taunting, laughter-filled eyes.

'It's mortifying,' she said and made her voice low and mournful. 'And the worst thing is, Dr Gallagher, that I've just realised I'm a born spinster.'

'"A born"...' Quinn folded his arms across his chest and his wicked eyes asked a million questions. 'Why?'

'Because Sam asked me if I'd poison people for him—or drown myself for love—and I've realised that I wouldn't do that for any man. No one!'

'Not even for me?'

The words caught her by surprise. Fern's eyes flashed up to his, expecting more laughter, but the laughter was softened by something behind his eyes that was deadly serious.

Fern's own laughter died.

'Not. . .not even for you, Quinn Gallagher,' she whispered, and her voice trembled.

'Not even a little bit? Not even a dose of Epsom salts in the punch to win your love?'

He sounded so disappointed that Fern almost choked. The laughter bubbled again, unbidden.

She fought for gravity—for some sort of control of a situation that was reeling way out of control.

'I thought you were going to bed,' she said darkly.

'I've told you.' Quinn's voice was mock innocent. 'I'm getting rid of your fiancé first. And then. . .'

And then. . .

Before she knew what he was about, Quinn stepped forward and caught her in his arms. She was ruthlessly kissed with a speed that left her gasping—that left her weak as butter in his hold—but was then released with equal speed.

It might never have happened.

Two seconds later Quinn was standing nonchalantly back against the wall as Geraldine swept around the corner. He looked for all the world like the cat that had won the cream—but to the passing nurse it could seem as if he hadn't touched anyone. . . Dr Gallagher and Dr Rycroft were indulging in formal conversation— no more. . .

'Now, about that future appointment. . .' Quinn said to Fern—his eyes wicked with laughter, his look delighting at the crimson suffusing her cheeks—and then turned his attention to Geraldine.

'Ah, Sister...' His voice was bland and impersonal. 'Looking for me?'

The nurse looked from Fern's crimson face to Quinn's bland one and back again and Fern knew that she wasn't totally deceived. The island would be buzzing with gossip by nightfall.

'The air ambulance has landed, Doctor,' the nurse said primly, her voice a little severe. She didn't like people trying to pull the wool over her eyes, Geraldine didn't. 'Is Mr Hubert ready?'

'I'll make sure he is.' Quinn pushed himself from lounging against the wall to an upright stance and straightened his white surgical coat. 'It's a serious duty—to get Mr Hubert off the island. Enough of this nonsense, Dr Rycroft,' he said sternly. 'You appear to be distracting me from my duty. There's work to be done.'

Enough of this nonsense...

While Quinn prepared Sam for travel and briefed the two doctors who had come on the plane to escort Sam to Sydney, Fern walked down and sat with her aunt.

Maud was sleeping.

Her aunt's obs were steady and her colour wasn't as bad as the day before but she certainly didn't look healthy.

What on earth would Maud say when she found out that Fern and Sam had broken their engagement?

She'd be heartbroken.

'I've just broken my promise to you,' Fern whispered down to her sleeping aunt, the consequences of the morning flooding in. 'How can I marry on the island now?'

There was one possibility that refused to be suppressed.

If she couldn't marry Sam, then who...?

Enough of this nonsense...

*   *   *

It took almost an hour before the air ambulance team were satisfied that Sam was stable enough to travel. Then he was carefully lifted out into Quinn's makeshift ambulance to be taken out to the airstrip.

Fern stood at the hospital entrance and watched him go.

'Good luck, Sam,' she whispered as he passed, reaching down to squeeze his hand in a grip of farewell.

Sam's eyes flicked open from his drug-induced sleep and he focused on her face.

'Fern...' He grabbed her hand hard and held it, making the two men carrying him pause.

'Fern, you know I can't marry you now,' he whispered.

'I know that.' Fern leaned over and kissed him lightly on the cheek. 'We never should have agreed to marry in the first place. We're friends, Sam. Just friends. I hope we always will be.'

'But, Fern...' Sam's grip still held tight. 'Your aunt...'

He'd remembered.

'She'll be fine,' Fern assured him, feeling far from sure herself. 'I'll persuade her to have the operation somehow.'

'You'll just have to marry another islander,' Sam muttered. 'Or how about marrying Dr Gallagher? He seems sweet on you!'

Even Sam had noticed, then.

There was a deathly silence.

Both ambulance bearers had heard, as had Lizzy walking beside the stretcher. And so had Quinn, following behind.

'Don't be silly, Sam,' Fern said and her voice was a trifle breathless.

'Yeah, Sam.' Lizzy was carrying a suitcase and sticking close by Sam's stretcher. She flashed a glance at Fern that was still a bit unsure—still a bit jealous. 'Don't be silly. I hope...I sure hope Fern does find someone... But it won't be Doc Gallagher.'

'Why not?' Argumentative as ever, Sam had his teeth in a good idea and he was sticking to it. 'Doc Gallagher seems a decent bloke and there's nothing wrong with our Fern.'

Our Fern. Islander talk.

Islander talk for one of them.

'Of course there's not,' Lizzy agreed kindly. She could afford to be generous now. 'But she still can't marry Dr Gallagher. How can she marry someone who's already married?'

Quinn married...

The group around the stretcher moved on and Fern stood aside to let them pass.

She stood absolutely still on the hospital steps as Quinn supervised Sam into the makeshift ambulance. Lizzy and the two doctors disappeared into its cavernous interior and Quinn closed the doors behind them.

He cast a doubtful look back at Fern.

Had he heard what Lizzy had said?

He must have. His doubtful look was for how Fern would take it.

There was no time for talk now. Quinn raised a hand in a gesture of farewell, swung into the driver's seat and then the ambulance and its load disappeared down the road toward the airstrip.

He'd be gone for twenty minutes or more.

Breathing time.

There was nothing to breathe for.

Still Fern didn't move. If someone was watching from the hospital windows they'd assume she was bereft—a white-faced girl staring after an ambulance as though it held everything she held most dear.

They'd assume she was grieving for Sam.

Married!

Her world tipped and tipped again.

Finally it came the right way up.

Lizzy might be wrong. Maybe Lizzy was making assumptions about Jessie—because they were sharing a house...

Slowly Fern turned and made her way through the house-cum-hospital to the kitchen.

Jessie was feeding her wallaby, the tiny wombat still an incongruous lump on her breast. She looked up as Fern walked in the door and smiled.

'OK?' she asked.

'OK.'

'You look...You look like you've just been kicked in the stomach.'

It was how she felt. Fern shook her head, trying to make her voice sound normal.

'Well, it's not every day I lose an intended husband...'

'Quinn said he didn't think you'd mind too much.'

'What would Quinn know?' Fern said savagely and turned away to the sink. She fiddled with taps and kettle, keeping her face carefully averted. 'Jess, is Quinn married?'

There was a long silence. It seemed that the room held its breath. All Fern could hear were the tiny gulping sounds made by the little joey as he sucked his milk—that and the sounds of her heart thumping against her breast.

'Why, yes, he is,' Jessie said at last, and Fern could tell by her voice that she was wondering why Fern was asking.

'Who...who is he married to?'

The silence deepened. Then Jessie carefully placed the little joey back into the pouch, bending carefully over him and just as carefully not looking at Fern.

'To me, of course,' she answered.

Of course.

There was no 'of course' about it, Fern thought miserably. Of course it was the obvious assumption when they were sharing a house but Quinn had carefully made it clear that they were separate right from the start.

They didn't share a bedroom. They'd split the house into his and hers and just shared a kitchen...

And a life.

There were marriages and marriages, Fern thought bleakly, but regardless of how separately they lived Jessie and Quinn were still man and wife.

Because they didn't share a bedroom—because Quinn was an arrant flirt—it didn't make them any less married.

Fern felt sick to the stomach. Her world was no longer tilting. It had shrivelled into something puckered and ugly and somehow...somehow tainted...

Numbly Fern gathered her bloodstained clothes from the night before and bade Jessie farewell.

This was where she bowed out.

She should go back to Sydney, she thought bleakly as she made her way out of the hospital, but her aunt was still desperately ill. There were fine strings of duty holding Fern to the island.

Not duty, Fern acknowledged at last, feeling the pain she had been trying to avoid since her family were killed.

She loved her aunt. She couldn't leave. The bonds of duty had become bonds of love.

She loved Quinn!

'I do not,' she said savagely to the silence as she started the long walk back to her uncle's farmhouse. Fern's car was still down at the harbour from last night and to have asked one of the hospital staff—or Jessie—for a ride would have choked her.

It was a half-hour walk. Fern kept off the road, knowing that Quinn would return this way from the airstrip.

She didn't want to see Quinn Gallagher ever again.

Quinn might be able to take his marriage vows lightly but if he did that... If he did that then how much truth was there in what he told her?

Somehow she had given her heart to a base cheat who was playing with the emotions of two women.

Two?

Who knew? There might even be more. Who knew what was causing those shadows under Jessie's eyes?

The girl looked haunted.

Fern thought back to the night before and mentally cringed. Quinn hadn't even let Fern go when Jessie walked in on them and he had put Fern to bed with all tenderness while Jessie was forced to watch.

'She doesn't have much time for people,' Quinn had said of his wife and Fern was starting to see why.

'He's a toad!' she said savagely to a lone cow peering over a fence. 'Toad, toad and double toad.'

The cow, heavy with calf and sleepy with the midday sun, closed her eyes and swayed as though she was in complete agreement.

How to get through the next few days?

How to persuade her aunt to leave the island?

There were no easy answers. Fern cleaned the house yet again for her uncle and then tackled his dry garden. The drought meant that there was no water for luxuries like watering the lawn so the front garden was a brown and dismal sight, but digging in the caked dirt was work suited to Fern's bruised soul—no matter how useless.

Finally, towards evening, when her uncle had disappeared again to visit his wife Fern donned her bathing suit and headed to the beach.

Beneath the house was a tiny cove. 'We had it put there just for you,' Fern's uncle had told her when Fern had first come to the island, and it was such a magic place—and so private—that Fern had almost believed him.

A tiny strip of soft white sand ran down to the water's edge. Out to sea a shelf of rocks deflected the worst of the surf so what had formed was a huge, natural swimming pool. Fern never swam alone. There were masses of glittering subtropical fish swimming beside her every stroke she took.

There was usually other company and tonight was no exception. Out to sea a pair of dolphins rolled lazily in the swell and then nosed their way in to find out who was intruding in their territory. The presence of the dolphins meant that sharks kept well away and the fluorescence of the leaping dolphins in the moonlight was enough to make Fern almost weep with their beauty.

Even the dolphins couldn't work their magic tonight, though.

Fern had come down here and swum and swum in the months after her parents' death, searching for some comfort in the steady rhythm of surf and sea and the companionship of the same two dolphins who seemed to use this cove as their permanent base. They had soothed her finally—but it had taken years.

Would it take years now?

Fern swam for what seemed an hour, until the sun was just a flickering memory of fire on the horizon.

Finally, reluctantly, she turned to shore.

Quinn was waiting.

How long he had been there she couldn't tell. He was sitting on the sand beside her towel, watching her with eyes that knew trouble when they saw it. His open-necked shirt was rippling in the soft night breeze, his jeans were rolled to the knees and his feet were bare.

His eyes never left Fern as she walked up the beach toward him.

Amazingly, there was compassion behind those dark eyes.

'I thought you'd turn to a prune,' he said gently, as she faltered and stopped. He stood and held out her towel. 'You and Lizzy... You're like fish...'

'Why are you here?'

It was a flat accusation and it cut across the night like a whip.

'I wanted to see you.'

'Well, you've seen me,' Fern snapped, snatching her towel from his hands and wrapping it round her wet bathing costume in a childish gesture of defence. 'Now leave.'

'What's wrong, my Fern?'

'I am not your Fern!' Fern turned away from him and stalked two yards up the path toward the house but suddenly she stopped, fury surging. She wheeled back to face him, green eyes flashing fore. 'How dare you make love to me, Quinn Gallagher? With Jessie present, even... How dare...?'

'I know why I dared,' Quinn said softly. He was watching her as a man might watch a dearly loved time bomb. He loved what he was seeing but he just knew that she was going to self-destruct.

So let her self-destruct...

'You're married to Jessie.' As explosive as any bomb, Fern's words shattered the peace of the cove. They echoed round and round them, awful in their truth.

There was a deathly silence.

'That's right,' Quinn said finally, as though confessing to something he had no part of. 'But that doesn't mean...'

'Doesn't mean what?' Fern asked in fury. 'Doesn't mean you can't have a bit on the side—and I'm the bit? And is Jessie supposed to sit back and watch? No wonder she looks like she has ghosts haunting her, Quinn Gallagher. With you as a husband, who needs ghosts?'

'Fern, you don't understand.' Quinn took a step towards her but Fern took a hasty step back. And another. 'It's just a marriage of convenience. Jess and I... We need to be married for all sorts of reasons—reasons I can't explain—but we're free to lead our own lives.'

'Well, from where I stand,' Fern said grimly, 'that looks like a really, really good deal for Quinn Gallagher. And a lousy one for Jess. But it doesn't matter, anyway, Dr Gallagher. I'm not the least bit interested in another woman's husband—even if I was interested in you in the first place. You've made me feel dirty. Jessie's lovely. She doesn't deserve my betrayal—as well as her husband's. You touch me once more and I'll scream sexual harassment so loud you'll hear it from the mainland. Now get off the beach before I start screaming.'

'Fern, you don't understand.'

'No?' Fern mocked, her anger building to the point where it was due to explode. 'You've got your lines wrong, Dr Gallagher. It's supposed to be "my wife doesn't understand me". Not "my latest floozie doesn't understand me".'

'"Floozie"...' Quinn's voice was blank.

'"Floozie",' Fern said through gritted teeth. 'Woman of ill repute. The sort of woman who makes love to others' husbands while wives are cringing in pain and mortification...' Fern took a deep breath.

'I can't apologise deeply enough to Jess for what I let happen between us. But I'm telling you now, Quinn Gallagher, whatever I feel—whatever I felt—nothing is going to happen between us again. Ever.'

'"Ever", Fern?' Quinn's voice was suddenly almost as desolate as hers.

There was real pain in his voice.

It took an iron will not to step towards the pain in Quinn's tone but somehow she found it.

'"Ever",' Fern whispered bleakly and turned to walk up the beach.

The hundred yards until she was out of sight were the longest hundred yards she had ever walked.

Quinn didn't follow.

CHAPTER EIGHT

THE news from Sydney the next morning was good.

Sam seemed on the way to recovery. He had tedious surgery in store to graft skin over the wound but his body was recovering from shock and his natural constitution of something akin to a very healthy ox was taking over.

Thanks to Quinn Gallagher's meticulous cleansing of the wound, there seemed no sign of infection.

Fern found some relief in the news of Sam—but not so much as would lift the black cloud of depression hanging over her.

The next two days seemed to take for ever.

Fern drifted from home to hospital in aimless misery, learning Quinn's clinic times and planning visits to her aunt purposefully to avoid him.

She was supposed to be on three weeks' honeymoon. Therefore she had three weeks of idleness before her, even if she went back to Sydney.

With someone else looking after her job in Sydney, there was no justification for Fern to leave her aunt and uncle—especially when they seemed to need her so much.

As Fern expected, Maud was appalled that Fern's engagement to Sam was off.

'Mind, it never really felt right,' she told her niece, gripping Fern's hand in trembling fingers. 'But I so hoped. . .'

'You so hoped to see me married,' Fern agreed. 'But maybe marrying isn't what I'm meant to do with my life.' She told her aunt Sam's logic—that Fern was clearly unsuitable because of her disinterest in drowning or poisoning—but it hardly cracked a smile.

'There'll be someone else in time.' Her aunt sighed. 'I just hope I'm alive to see it.'

'You will be if you have this operation.'

'I don't know.' Fern's aunt sank back onto the pillows and a tear of hopelessness slid down the pillows. 'I thought I might hold your wedding out as a bribe. I don't know whether I can make you understand, Fern, but it felt like a sort of a bribe to me. If I agreed to the operation then nice things would happen as well as scary ones.'

'They will,' Fern said with asperity. 'For a start, you'll live.'

'But that's in the future.' Her aunt sniffed at her crazy logic and shook her head. 'I suppose you'll talk me into it eventually,' she whispered, 'but for now... leave me be, Fern. I just want to sleep.'

She was growing weaker.

She should be in Sydney now, Fern thought bleakly, wishing that there was some way she could forcibly pick her aunt up and move her. Impossible. To take her without her full co-operation—without her calm acceptance of what was happening—would be to put more strain on her damaged heart. The results could be disastrous.

She left her aunt soon after.

'Dr Gallagher wants to see you,' Geraldine told Fern as she left her aunt's room. 'He asked you to wait.'

'If Dr Gallagher wishes to discuss my aunt then he'd better do it with my uncle,' Fern said bleakly, 'because I don't want to discuss anything at all with Dr Gallagher.'

She walked out with her head high and, ignoring Geraldine's astonished look, climbed into her car and burst into tears.

Her nights were awful.

Fern took hours to drift into troubled sleep and the nightmares she had made it hardly worth the effort. When her uncle woke her that night it took a while to realise that his calls weren't an extension of her dreadful dreams.

'Fern!'

Her uncle's voice finally penetrated the mist. Fern sat up in bed, fumbling for the light switch and for reality.

'Fern!' There was trouble in her uncle's voice—and urgency.

Her aunt. Something was wrong with her aunt. Even as Fern stumbled out of bed the nightmares cemented into certainty and she knew what the matter was. Her aunt had died and someone had telephoned from the hospital. She'd been so exhausted that she hadn't heard. . .

By the time she reached the head of the stairs the horror inside her was a sick dread. Fern stared down the stairs at her uncle's face in the hall light, waiting for confirmation.

It wasn't there. Her uncle's face didn't reflect her horror.

It wasn't Maud, then. . .

It was something urgent, but not with Al's beloved wife.

'What's wrong?' Fern managed, relief making her dizzy.

'Fern, how do you feel about getting dressed and coming on a mercy mission?'

Fern shook the last strands of nightmare away with a visible effort.

'A. . .mercy mission?'

'Look, it may be nothing,' her uncle confessed, 'but I can't help feeling a bit concerned. . .'

'About my aunt?'

'No.' The elderly farmer shook his head. 'Maybe I'm being a fool—but I was worrying about Maud and couldn't sleep so I went down to the kitchen to make myself a cup of tea. You can see Bill Fennelly's place from the kitchen. His light's still on.'

'So?'

Bill Fennelly was a neighbour, a man in his twenties, and he'd lived alone since his sister married. He was asthmatic, Fern remembered. His asthma was sometimes severe but the last time Fern had seen him he'd been well enough. Had she seen him the day of the wedding? She couldn't remember. Maybe she hadn't seen him since the last time she'd been home—twelve months ago.

'I guess he's just reading a good book,' she suggested mildly but her uncle shook his head.

'He's been crook, Fern. He had pneumonia just before you came home. It took ages to clear. I know Doc Gallagher's still worried about him, though. He checked him at home a couple of days ago and wanted to stick him in hospital but Bill wouldn't have a bar of it. He's fed up to the back teeth with being ill. And I saw him earlier tonight down at the store. He's looking bloody awful—worse than Maud—and coughing fit to bust. Said he was going straight home to bed—but now the light's still on.'

'So he went to sleep with the light on.'

'You don't know Bill Fennelly,' her uncle said darkly. 'Comes from a very parsimonious line, does our Bill. No Fennelly known to man has ever gone to sleep with the light on.'

'We could telephone,' Fern said doubtfully. 'It couldn't hurt.'

'I already have.' Al Rycroft lifted his coat from the hook by the door. 'There's no answer. So I'm going over. I'd appreciate your company—but I'll go alone if you won't come.'

'Oh, of course I'll come.' Fern took a deep breath. 'Of course.'

Bill was an islander. The islanders looked after their own—and Fern was an islander as well.

Whether she liked it or not.

Bill's house was locked and silent when they approached. Bill Fennelly was the only son of dour, strict parents and little had been wasted on luxuries. The farmhouse had always been bleak, though Fern noticed that a bright row of roses had been newly planted by the front door. Breaking out, our Bill, since his parents' death.

They knocked and knocked again and then Al stood back and lobbed stones up at the bedroom window. No one appeared.

'The man must be dead,' Al said morosely. 'The din we've made is enough to wake an army.'

'Maybe we should contact Quinn,' Fern said uneasily.

'Why?' Al had disappeared into the dark back shed with his torch. Now he reappeared carrying a crowbar. 'We have the means to get in and there's a qualified doctor on hand. What more could we ask?'

'That we know he's home. Uncle, what are you intending to do with that thing?'

'Smash the door in.'

'And if he's gone to his sister's for the night because he's not feeling well?'

Al paused. 'You know, I never thought of that, Fern, girl,' he said solemnly. 'I hope you're right. Guess I'll help Bill fix the door in the morning if he's done that.'

'Wouldn't it be better to check first?'

'Not now we're here.'

He'd had enough talking. Al had decided to see for himself long before waking Fern and nothing was stopping him now.

He placed the crowbar against the lock and shoved. Then shoved again.

The old wood creaked a protest and then splintered into fragments as the door folded inwards.

Bill hadn't gone to his sister's.

He was lying on the kitchen floor, his face grey, and the floor tiles under his head were specked scarlet. He'd been coughing blood but he was almost past coughing now. Every breath was a frantic, rasping effort.

He was facing the door as they entered and Fern saw relief flooding through the fear.

Thank heaven for Al's decisiveness.

'What the hell's wrong?'

Al bent over Bill and took his shoulder. 'What is it, mate?'

Bill didn't answer. He couldn't. Al looked frantically up at Fern but Fern was raking the kitchen with her eyes. Most severe asthmatics had salbutomol, pump and nebuliser close at hand—in case. If ever there was an 'in case' this was it.

'Where's your stuff, Bill?' she snapped across his dreadful breathing. 'Here or in the bedroom?'

Bill rolled his eyes upward and then went on to fighting for all that mattered. His life.

Fern raced up the stairs three at a time. What she needed was laid out in neat preparation on the bedroom dresser.

It might as well have been on the moon as far as Bill was concerned. In his condition, Bill could no more climb the stairs than fly.

Fern was near flying, though. The strain on Bill's system from that frantic effort to breathe couldn't last much longer.

In seconds she was back downstairs, fitting Bill's mask over his face as she squatted down beside him.

'OK, Bill,' she said gently. 'We're here now and we won't let you die.' It must have been the most terrifying of experiences, she thought grimly, to feel yourself getting worse by the minute and yet not be able to call for help.

There were things that didn't make sense. Surely the asthma hadn't hit so suddenly that Bill hadn't time to locate his salbutamol and mask. Experienced asthmatics knew when an attack was starting. And why was he coughing blood?

She placed her hand on his forehead and winced. His temperature was sky-high.

A return of the pneumonia?

'We need to get you to hospital, Bill,' she said briefly. Her uncle had his car outside. 'We'll take you now.'

'You don't reckon we ought to get Doc Gallagher with his ambulance?' Al asked uneasily.

Fern shook her head. 'Ring and let him know we're coming,' she ordered. 'But the sooner I get Bill into a hospital bed the happier I'll be. OK, Bill?'

Bill's hand came up to clutch her arm and the expression on his face was one of wholehearted agreement.

Quinn was waiting for them.

Al's phone call had elucidated three short, sharp questions and then a command.

'Get him in fast.'

Al had done as ordered, driving like a maniac with his hand on the horn and, Fern suspected, rather enjoying the drama.

Fern hadn't. She'd sat in the back seat with her young neighbour, holding the mask and attempting reassurance, and all the while asking herself what could be wrong.

Bill was three years younger than Fern but she knew him well. He'd always had asthma but it hadn't seemed to slow him down. He played football and cricket and put in a hard day's labour with the best of them. Now, though...

Now Bill's big frame seemed to have shrunk. Fern's arm was around his chest, supporting him, and it seemed that he must have shed almost half his weight.

Pneumonia... This weight loss didn't fit with one bout of pneumonia and then a relapse. It was more typical of terminal cancer.

Quinn would have eluded cancer—surely. So what was going on?

Legionella? AIDS? Psittacosis?

He didn't seem a candidate for any of those things— but who knew?

Possible diagnoses were still running through her head as the car screeched to a halt and Quinn hauled open the back door.

He had oxygen ready. Quinn's mask replaced Fern's in seconds and Fern moved swiftly to assist in lifting the absurdly light farmer to a stretcher.

She'd have to stay. A quick glance at Quinn had found his face grim and drawn and maybe she had something to do with that but the situation Quinn was facing with Bill was enough to make any doctor look grim.

This was no ordinary asthma attack.

For the first time, Fern found herself feeling what it must be like to be a lone doctor in a place like this. There was no fall-back position at all—except for a plane to take patients to the mainland in dire emergencies. The plane couldn't get here for hours and even then patients could choose not to go. Many of the islanders chose just that.

Like Aunt Maud...

'I'll live and die on the island, thank you very much. I don't want mainlanders muddling my insides with heaven knows what.'

How many times had Fern heard words like that from elderly islanders, even when there was no doctor on the island at all.

Quinn Gallagher was therefore a heaven-sent blessing for the islanders. Even if he was a toad, at least he was a medically competent toad.

'What's happening here?' Fern asked softly as together they pushed the trolley down the corridor. 'Do you have any idea what's going on?'

Quinn glanced down at Bill and his face set, if possible growing even grimmer. 'God knows,' he said frankly. 'Bill's been ill for months—though never so critically as this. I'd appreciate a bit of your time here, Dr Rycroft.'

She couldn't refuse. Given the same scenario, Fern would be terrified.

A critically ill man with no clear diagnosis...

In Sydney she'd call in the big guns. The top physicians.

Here there was Quinn and Fern.

'I'll wait for you outside, Fern,' Al said unsteadily. Fern's uncle had been steering at the foot of the stretcher while Fern walked beside Quinn at the head. At the door to the ward he stopped dead.

'No need. I'll run Fern home—or one of the nurses will,' Quinn said shortly, and Al cast Quinn a look of real gratitude.

He'd done his duty. Now he wanted out.

Fern couldn't protest. She couldn't be concerned that she was forced to spend yet more time with Quinn Gallagher.

The tension between Fern and Quinn had to be put aside. Bill's needs took precedence. He was losing ground. Even after five minutes of oxygen the young farmer appeared cyanosed and limp.

'Adrenaline, I think,' Quinn muttered, his hands already adjusting tubing.

'I'll do it.'

Thankfully, emergency trays were set up the same everywhere. Whoever had set the standards knew what they were doing. It meant that a doctor strange to a hospital could work at almost maximum efficiency straight away.

She reached for the syringe and her uncle blenched.

'See you at home, Fern,' Al muttered and bolted.

Fern's escape route was cut.

Fern had to fight an almost overwhelming urge to bolt right after her uncle.

She had to stay. She and Quinn were Bill's lifeline. She had no choice.

It was a good two hours before Bill decided to live—for the moment—and at the end of that time Fern was exhausted. Her skills had been stretched to the limit and the fact that Bill was a childhood friend didn't help one bit.

Finally, Bill drifted into a near-normal sleep, his breath still rasping and laboured but at least it was steady.

'For now,' Quinn said bitterly as they left the ward. The night sister was sitting by the bed and would stay there until morning. 'The pneumonia's obviously taken hold again—but why? Why?'

They were walking slowly down the corridor together, the tension between them put aside as both concentrated on Bill's plight.

'Malignancy?' Fern suggested and Quinn shook his head.

'There's no sign. When Bill started losing weight I persuaded him to spend a couple of days in Sydney. I gave the radiologists carte blanche to find anything— and there was nothing. The antibiotic stops the pneumonia but this is the third bout he's had. There has to be an underlying cause.'

He paused and dug his hands deep in his pockets. The lights in the corridor were dimmed but the strain around Quinn's eyes was still obvious. He looked exhausted, Fern thought, her image of the indefatigable Dr Gallagher who never needed sleep fading fast. Now he leaned back against the corridor wall and ran his hand through his hair in a gesture of absolute exhaustion.

'When Bill was in Sydney I had a physician look at him,' Quinn continued. 'He suggested Bill's only problem was mycoplasma pneumonia and I hadn't left him on antibiotics long enough the last time he'd had it. He's been on antibiotics almost continually since then, though, and here he is crook again. I guess. . .I guess I should send him back to Sydney. Trouble is, I reckon the next we'll hear of Bill will be of his death. The Sydney physicians don't seem to have any more of a clue than I have.'

And his death would hurt, Fern knew, looking up at Quinn's defeated face. This man might be a cheat to the women in his life but there was no doubting that he was a caring doctor.

He was worried sick now.

'What's causing the haemoptysis?' she asked slowly. The plugs of bloody phlegm Bill was coughing were not normal for straight pneumonia.

'The coughing might be causing it—or the continued infection.' Quinn shrugged. 'His cough's so dry and consistent that he could be breaking small blood vessels. There hasn't been much haemoptysis till now.'

'There was a fair bit tonight.' Fern frowned. 'You've excluded things like AIDS?'

'Of course.' Quinn wasn't offended. He seemed almost grateful to go through the options with another doctor and Fern knew how he was feeling. There was nothing worse than not knowing what was wrong when you were the only one qualified to do anything about it.

Quinn lifted a hand and wearily counted on his fingers. 'It's not HIV, or Q fever, or legionella or psittacosis. A CT scan of the thorax and abdomen were normal. Mycoplasma and Brucella serology were normal. He's been on Aminophylline twice a day and bronchodilator and steroid inhalers for his asthma, and until six months ago his asthma was well controlled. It certainly isn't now. He's lost over four stone and is still losing. His sputum grows only a light growth of beta haemolytic Strep Group D and at last count his white cells were 7.38.'

Fern stared. For a country GP without specialist internal medicine training, Quinn's search for a diagnosis was impressive.

But not conclusive.

There had to be something else.

'Have you excluded TB?' asked Fern thoughtfully. TB was rare in this country now—but not unheard-of. Mostly it occurred in migrants coming from more heavily infested areas, in AIDS sufferers or in elderly derelicts whose general poor health made then susceptible. Bill was certainly none of these.

'His Mantoux test showed a positive response,' Quinn told her. 'But we've sent off pleural aspirate for cytology with negative results. Pleural biopsy, bronchoscopy and bronchial washings have all shown nothing. If I send him to Sydney now, the hospital's going to waste time repeating all those tests and meanwhile...'

'Meanwhile he'll be dead,' Fern said brutally. 'We've run out of time for tests.'

'Bill's run out of time for living, then.'

'Maybe.'

Fern scuffed her toe on the polished wood of the corridor, a habit she'd started as a child when she was thinking hard.

Silence.

'He's running a fair temperature,' she said at last.

'He has all along. Even when we cleared the pneumonia he's been spiking nocturnal temperatures of thirty nine plus,' Quinn told her. 'I saw him the day after your...after your attempt at a wedding...because I was concerned he might have eaten some of those damned oysters.

'In fact, he hadn't eaten any because he was feeling off colour, anyway. He hadn't tried to go to your wedding. I thought his temp was up then—but he wouldn't come in for a check. Said he was as well as he'd been for a month and he was sick to death of being prodded and poked. I can't say I blame him.'

'But his Mantoux test showed positive...'

'Half the population of the known world shows a positive Mantoux test,' Quinn said brutally. 'That doesn't mean he's consumptive.'

'It means TB hasn't been excluded, though...'

'The tests were negative...'

'They often come back with false negatives.' Fern's sandal scraped forward and back again. Her personal friction with Quinn was forgotten for the moment. Her mind was all on long-ago lectures.

'Sometimes asthma treatments can stir up TB,' she said thoughtfully. 'It's been documented.'

'Yeah?' Quinn was watching Fern's face, trying to follow her thought processes. There was no denigration of a junior doctor here. If Fern had an idea that might help, Quinn Gallagher wanted to hear it.

'It's true. And somewhere. . .I remember one of my professors saying over and over, ''Never let a patient die with an undiagnosed fever without at least considering TB and a trial of triple therapy''. He was an elderly professor who'd seen a lot of TB—but his advice is still sound. He didn't trust tests. He trusted what his gut feeling was telling him.'

'So. . .' Quinn was still noncommittal, still watching.

'So we either give up on Bill and send him to Sydney,' Fern said. 'And hope he survives the trip. Or we treat the pneumonia aggressively and at the same time we start him on treatment for TB. My gut feeling's saying TB and I think we should go with that. We send more pleural fluid for culture but even if that comes back negative we keep him on the regime for a while— just to see.'

'But if we're not sure. . .'

'Are we sure it's anything else?'

'No. But. . .'

'Then what's our choice here, Dr Gallagher?'

Quinn stared at the girl in front of him as if he was seeing her for the first time. Fern's voice was steady. This was a considered choice and she was ready to accept the consequences if it failed.

'What on earth's your training?' he asked. 'I asked your aunt if you'd done anaesthetics and she said you'd done a resident rotation—but you don't talk like any intern I've ever met.'

Fern smiled faintly and shook her head. 'I'm a specialist medical registrar,' she admitted. 'I've done my first part of internal medicine. In twelve months I'll be a qualified physician.'

'A physician. . .' Quinn's eyes widened. 'For

heaven's sake. . .' He shook his head as if in disbelief. 'You realise—once you're fully trained—what we could offer here. . .?'

' "We"?'

' "We",' Quinn said, his voice firming as the ramifications hit home. 'Fern, I'm a surgeon and I'm trained for accident and emergencies. You have enough anaesthetic training to support me—and you're a physician, for heaven's sake. . .'

'Not yet.'

'No. But if we found a locum to take over here. . . Dr Rycroft, all we lack is an obstetrician. With the hospital already operating and if the job was advertised only for twelve months we'd find a locum to take over from us. There are medicos who'd see twelve months here as a welcome break, as long as they weren't pressured to stay at the end of it.

'If we were to spend twelve months in Sydney— you finishing your physician training while I deliver every baby I can get my hands on and getting myself some paediatric training in the process—think of the service we could offer.'

'And Jessie would come back to Sydney with us while we did it, I suppose?' Fern said slowly, watching his face.

Quinn shook his head. 'She'd stay here.'

'Without her husband?'

The word hit Quinn almost as a physical slap. He took a step back and stared down at Fern.

His burst of enthusiasm faded and fatigue crept back.

'Jessie wouldn't mind,' he said flatly.

'Well, I'd mind for Jess.' Somehow Fern made her voice brisk and businesslike but it wasn't how she was feeling. 'Do you want help writing up a drug list for Bill?' she asked harshly. 'If so, let's do it and then ask someone to take me home. I really have other things to do than stand in hospital corridors and discuss plans by you to abandon someone who clearly loves you.'

* * *

The drug regime was tricky.

Fern had treated little TB in the past. It took time to sort through the texts and pharmaceutical lists and find just what she wanted.

Quinn deferred to her.

'If I have a road crash to deal with then I'll expect you to take orders from me, Dr Rycroft,' he said brusquely, pointedly formal after Fern's snapping rebuff. 'This is internal medicine, though—and I know when to stand aside.'

With his medicine he knew when to stand aside, Fern thought grimly. With little else.

She reacted by ignoring him, preparing her list in grim silence.

Finally she finished and rose from the desk. He was still watching her—as a hungry cat watches a mouse—and Fern didn't like it one bit.

'I'll drive you home,' he said firmly.

'And if Bill has a relapse?'

'I'll check him on the way but if his breathing's settled he's hardly going to wake and choke in the time it takes to get you home. The nurse will stay with him and I have the phone on my belt. I can get back fast.'

'What about...What about the night sister taking me home—and leaving you here?'

'What about the night sister?' Quinn's brows arched and for a moment Fern saw a trace of the old humour. 'Sister Haynes doesn't drive anything more powerful than a bicycle—and Jessie's asleep. So it's my offer or nothing.'

'I'll walk.'

'You want to come peacefully or forcibly?' Quinn asked politely, and through the exhaustion the laughter was back with a vengeance.

'Is that a threat?'

'How can you doubt me, Dr Rycroft?' Quinn demanded, wounded that she had so little faith. 'Of course it is.'

* * *

It was a charmed night.

If the island didn't get rain soon the farmers would be in serious trouble, Fern knew, but it was hard to think about that on a night as perfect as tonight.

If Quinn wasn't married it would be magic indeed.

Quinn was married, though. Fern sat as far away from him as possible, hunched over against the door as if she was afraid.

She was.

She was afraid of her own feelings. She'd never felt like this about a man before and to feel this way about someone who was living with his wife...

Quinn stayed silent, his face set and grim. From time to time he glanced across at the girl by his side but he said nothing until he pulled to a halt outside her uncle's house and Fern put her hand on the doorhandle.

The doorhandle wouldn't budge. The central locking had been activated.

'Do you mind?' Fern said icily. 'Let me out.'

'Not until you've talked things through with me for a little.' Quinn glanced at his watch. 'Fern, hear me out. I can't be away from the hospital for long. You know that. I'm not about to make love to you—though God knows I want to. If I did you could scream loud enough from here to make your uncle hear. I just want to talk.'

Fern took a deep breath. Her fingers clenched into her palms.

'So talk.'

'That's what I like about you, Dr Rycroft,' Quinn said evenly, the laughter surfacing. 'You're always so amenable to suggestion.'

'Just get on with it.'

He didn't.

Instead, Quinn put his hands on the steering wheel and stared out into the night.

The laughter faded.

It was as if Quinn Gallagher was fighting some

unpleasant internal battle and Fern just had to wait for the outcome.

She watched him and her anger slowly disappeared as she did. Fern's fingers unclenched. She didn't know what was going on—but she couldn't maintain rage against this man. No matter how important it was that she did. . .

'Fern, I want you to reconsider staying on the island,' Quinn said at last. 'It makes sense to everyone that you stay. Most of all, it makes sense to me.'

'Not to me it doesn't.'

'Would it make a difference if I told you I'd fallen in love with you?'

Quinn didn't turn to her. His eyes were still staring out through the windscreen at the black of the night road. 'I fell for a bride in white satin,' he went on softly, and it was as if he was talking to the night—not to Fern. 'The most frightened bride I've ever seen, and the most beautiful. I was hit by bridal fever, you might say. It hit hard and since then I've been trying to find a cure. There isn't one.'

'I don't believe you,' Fern whispered. 'You don't fall in love like that.'

'Oh, yes, you do,' Quinn said grimly. 'I didn't ask for it to happen. I went to your wedding out of social obligation to your aunt and uncle—nothing else—and then I saw you. . .'

He turned to her then but still he didn't touch her. Quinn Gallagher was holding himself back with an iron will.

'Are you saying you don't feel this, too?' Quinn asked gently, and the gentleness in Quinn's voice was close to Fern's undoing. 'Because I don't believe you. You looked at me in that church and whatever hit, it hit both of us—with just as much force as those damned oysters. Only the effects are much more long-lasting—aren't they, Fern?'

'The effects just mean I have to get back to

Sydney—fast,' Fern whispered. 'Surely you can see that?'

'You mean you can feel it, too?' There was a trace of relief in Quinn's voice as though he'd been sure—but not too sure.

'Oh, I can feel animal attraction,' Fern said bitterly. 'But that's all this is. We'd go to bed and it'd be over in a week.'

'Want to try and see?'

'Don't be ridiculous.' Fern's face whitened and her fingers clenched again. 'Quinn Gallagher, are you or are you not married to Jessie?'

There was a long, long silence. Quinn Gallagher was facing some sort of internal war and when it was over the defeat was back in his voice.

'Jessie's and my marriage is in name only.'

'But she's here, she's still your wife and she has no intention of leaving the island. Where does that leave me in your plans, Dr Gallagher? A bit on the side—or are you planning on installing me as second bride?'

'Jessie understands. She knows how I feel. Believe me, Fern. . . Or if you won't believe me, ask Jess.'

'Oh, sure.' Fern thought back to Jessie's white, shadowed face and mentally cringed. 'Sure. Go and talk to Jessie. Ask her if she'd mind if I took over her husband. . .You've got rocks in your head. She's a lovely, gentle person, Quinn Gallagher. She doesn't deserve you.'

'The marriage is finished.'

Fern shrugged. 'There's a law in Australia,' she said conversationally. 'It's that married couples have to separate for at least twelve months before they can divorce. *Separate*, Dr Gallagher. Live in different houses. Have you any intention of doing that?'

'We can't,' Quinn said heavily. 'You must be able to see that.'

'I don't think I can see very much at all,' Fern whispered, her voice breaking. 'I don't understand. I don't understand what you're saying we should do. I don't understand what I'm feeling. I only know...I only know that I have to get away fast. I can't cope...' She struggled with the doorhandle. 'Quinn, unlock the door. Let me go—please...'

'Let you go?' he said dully. He shook his head. 'I told you, Fern. What I've caught is incurable. I'll let you get out of the car—even go back to Sydney—but I can never let you go.'

He lifted his hand and touched her hair, as if he were touching a dear and fragrant memory. His eyes held the same bleakness and loss as a man looking at a lost love.

'You'd better go, Fern,' he said bleakly. 'But not, please God, not for ever...'

CHAPTER NINE

FERN spent the night staring sleeplessly at the ceiling—and making some very hard decisions.

The next morning she again waited until Quinn was safely in Clinic and then returned to the hospital.

She visited Bill first.

The young man was sleeping deeply, obviously exhausted from the previous night's drama.

To Fern's relief his asthma seemed to have settled and he was breathing with relative ease. The dry, hacking cough was still there, though. It shook his body as he slept and his pillow was specked with blood.

She had to be right, Fern thought grimly. If she wasn't...

She must be.

She lifted the chart from the end of the bed. Bill's temperature was still high but it was too early to expect the pneumonia treatment to be working. It was TB... If they could keep him alive for the course of treatment to take effect...

It was Bill's only chance at life.

Quinn was following her advice to the letter.

For one crazy moment Fern let her mind drift. What if... What if she considered Quinn's mad proposal? She and Quinn running this hospital. Together...

With Jessie in the background!

'Don't be a fool,' she said harshly to herself. Her decision had been made.

She left Bill without waking him.

Aunt Maud was propped up on pillows in the next ward, a magazine lying on the coverlet in front of her. She wasn't reading, though. Maud lay staring out of the windows at the distant sea, as though soaking up every inch of view she could get.

Impulsively Fern crossed to the windows, throwing them wide to let the smell of the sea permeate the room.

Her aunt sighed with pleasure.

'I wanted to do that myself, Fern, dear,' she admitted, 'but it seemed too much effort to get out of bed.'

Fern sighed. 'Aunt, you must have the bypass surgery,' she said softly. She walked back to the bed and took her aunt's hands. 'There's no choice. The way it's looking—well, to be blunt, I don't like your chances of coming home unless you do.'

Her aunt nodded. 'I know that.' Maudie looked again out to sea. 'I just wish. . .'

Fern stooped to give her aunt a swift hug. 'You just wish it'll all be here waiting when you get back. The sea. The island. They will be. I promise.'

'And you? Fern, why won't you come home?'

Silence.

Fern stepped back from the bed, searching for something to say. There were slow tears of distress and weakness sliding down her aunt's cheeks.

'I did come home,' Fern whispered. 'I always come home for visits. And I'll take you to Sydney and then I'll bring you back again. I promise.'

'And leave again.'

'I can't practise here,' Fern said gently. 'Even if I wanted to now, I can't. Dr Gallagher is the island doctor.'

'He says he's asked you to be his partner.'

Fern bit her lip. 'Has he also told you he's married?'

Fern's aunt sniffed into a tissue, pulling herself back to her normal prosaic self with a visible effort. 'Well, of course, he's married,' she said bluntly. 'Jessie's a lovely girl, too, even if she is painfully shy. But Fern, Dr Gallagher being married shouldn't stop you being his partner. That's silly.'

Silly. . .

She supposed it was.

The whole darned thing was silly. Silly to the point of hysterical!

'Staying here's impossible,' Fern said at last. 'Believe me, Auntie. . .'

'Because we haven't healed you. . .'

Fern's eyes widened. 'I don't. . .I don't know what you mean.'

Maud sighed. 'Oh, Fern, we did so want children, your uncle and I. And when your parents were killed—well, we thought, at least we'd have a daughter. Someone we could love like our own. Selfish, really. Only. . .only we never really reached you. You've put up barriers so high. . .Fern, you've built those barriers and we can't get through. No one can. It tears us in two—your uncle and I. . .'

Fern swallowed. 'I. . . But I do love you,' she said softly. 'You know I do.'

'But you won't depend on us,' Maud said. 'The giving always has to be on your side. You won't take. You think if you take, then you expose yourself to hurt again. You won't take our love. . .'

'I do. . .'

'You don't,' Maud said gently. 'And what I'm really fearful of, my Fern, is that you won't take anyone's. Are you going to depend on anyone, Fern—ever?'

'I guess. . .I guess I have to say I hope not,' Fern said, struggling to keep her voice light. If Maud only knew. . . If her aunt guessed how much her niece had changed in the few short days since the fiasco of a wedding. . .

All she wanted to do now was depend on someone—on Quinn Gallagher—for the rest of her life. She wanted interdependence like she wanted life itself. Two made one. . .

For the first time in her life, Fern was guessing what the words of the marriage ceremony really meant.

'Will you come to Sydney and have this operation?' Fern asked steadily, avoiding her aunt's troubled eyes and changing the subject back to something safer. 'The passenger plane comes in on Friday. We could organise your transport on that. I'll stay with you all the time. I promise.'

'But. . .'

'But I thought about it last night—and I've decided to leave on Friday, regardless, Auntie Maud. But I think you should come with me.'

Maud sighed.

'You'll leave, anyway?'

'I must.'

Silence.

'And if I don't?' Maud whispered into the silence.

'Then you'll die.' There was no point in promising anything else. Not with a heart as damaged as Maud's.

'But you're not going to marry Sam.'

'No.'

Her aunt sighed once more.

'All right, Fern.'

Fern's aunt closed her eyes as though she was in pain. She bit her lip. 'I'll come with you and have this dratted operation,' she said sadly. 'Even if it kills me. Your promise still holds good, though, Fern. When you marry, you marry on the island. I'm holding you to that.'

'I don't. . .' It was better to be honest—wasn't it? 'I don't think I'll marry.'

Her aunt shook her head sadly. 'Fern, love—no matter what happens to me. . .remember. . .'

' "Remember"?'

'It's easier to give than receive,' Maud whispered harshly. 'You give and give and give. . .but if you don't learn it has to be both ways, then you'll never be happy. Sam wasn't the man for you, dear, and you know that. The next man who comes along. . . Well, I'm agreeing to this operation because I don't want to hurt your uncle with my death. I don't mind so much for me—but we depend on each other. I need him and I know he needs me. Open yourself to that sort of love, Fern, dear. Try. . .'

Fern swallowed.

'I'll try,' she whispered and she knew she was lying as deeply as she'd ever lied before.

She was trying desperately not to try at all.

Jessie met her on the way out of the hospital. The vet came running down the hospital steps to catch Fern before she pulled out of the hospital car park.

'Fern, stop. I've been waiting for you,' Jess called. Fern was already in the car but she paused and opened the car window when Jessie blocked her path. 'Please... Please, I need to talk to you.'

'I was just going home to make my uncle lunch,' Fern said doubtfully, glancing at her watch. If she stayed longer she risked meeting Quinn as he finished morning clinic. Then, at the look on Jessie's face, she relented. Jessie seemed almost pleading.

There was something different about Jessie this morning.

Jessie's third breast had disappeared.

'You've had a mastectomy,' Fern teased, forcing lightness as she followed the girl back into the hospital. Then she winced at the look of distress flooding Jessie's face.

'My little wombat died this morning,' Jess said sadly. 'He never really stood a chance. He was shocked—and I think he'd been out of the pouch for some hours before he was found. He was badly dehydrated and needed antibiotics but I couldn't get the mix right. Finally his diarrhoea was so bad his bowel ulcerated. The ulcers burst and he bled to death.'

Fern grimaced. The mixed blessings of medicine! It was the hardest lesson of being a doctor—that there were times when you just couldn't win.

'Do you know why he was out of his mum's pouch?' she asked gently. 'Was his mum injured?'

'I don't know.' Jessie was leading the way through the hospital corridor into the kitchen as she talked, ignoring Fern's obvious reluctance. 'Actually, they're the babies that are the hardest ones to save—when there's no obvious reason for them being abandoned. Even if I get them to adulthood, often I find something wrong—some defect that the mother sensed but I didn't. This one may have been dumped for such a reason.'

'So you've been awake nights for nothing,' Fern ventured, seeing the deepening of the shadows on Jessie's face.

'I wouldn't say that.' Jessie stooped down and lifted the little wallaby Fern had helped Quinn feed from his pouch by the stove. 'At least I tried. And I'm succeeding with this one. You don't mind if I feed while I talk?'

'Go right ahead.' Fern sat down at the kitchen table and found herself immediately holding an armful of blanketed joey.

'Quinn tells me you're an expert already.' Jess gave a forced smile. 'If you feed Walter while I talk then I can prepare formula for my echidna at the same time.' She handed over the tiny plastic bottle. 'All yours, Dr Rycroft.'

It was all Walter's. The joey saw the bottle coming, opened his mouth and sucked with fury. He nestled back in Fern's arms in contented bliss while Jessie fiddled with mixtures on the bench.

It was as if she was buying time.

Fern watched, forcing herself to be patient, as Jessie finished stirring her formula, placed it in the fridge and then lifted a can of cat food from the shelf.

'Cat food?' Fern queried faintly. 'Surely you don't have a cat? There's not one on the island—is there?'

'It's for my little rosella,' Jessie told her, gesturing to the young parrot in the cage in the corner. 'I use cat food and high protein baby cereal in equal proportions, mixed with a little calcium and multi-vitamin drops. It feeds him beautifully.'

'So what medical textbook does that come from?'

'No book, unfortunately,' Jessie grimaced. 'Trial and error.' Jessie crossed to the cage and opened it, lifting the little parrot out and gently offering it the food. The rosella knew what was coming. The food went into his crop easily: he swallowed and looked for more.

Whatever Jessie wanted was taking a long time to surface.

'Why did you want to see me?' Fern said at last. Jessie's back was to her, her attention seemingly all on the rosella, and Fern couldn't see her face. She sensed tension, though—tension and distress.

'Quinn says...Quinn says he's asked you to stay—and you won't because of me.'

Fern drew in her breath. Jess was still turned away, her shoulders hunched in misery, and Fern's heart turned over.

How could Quinn do this?

'That's not true,' Fern said steadily. 'Quinn's your husband, Jess. He has no right...no right at all to say that to you. It's horrid and hurtful and...and it's just not true.' Her voice trailed off to nothing.

'It's not like... It's not like we've a normal marriage,' Jess whispered sadly, as though she hadn't heard what Fern had said. The rosella was back on his perch and she stroked him with a gentle finger. 'Quinn and I... Well, we've been friends for ever. He was my cousin before we married. And the marriage... Well, it seemed like an extension of the friendship, really. We do everything separately, though, Fern. If he wanted...if he wants to be with you then I don't have the right...I don't have the right to stop him.'

'You do have the right,' Fern said savagely. The tiny joey started in her arms and she forced her voice to remain even. 'Quinn's your husband. He's not my husband. He doesn't want to divorce you—does he?'

'No.' Jess shook her head. 'But there are reasons,' she said miserably. 'There are reasons why we can't divorce—yet. He wouldn't have told me about you except I guessed. I've never seen him lit up like this before, Fern. Like he's alive. He's not like that with me.'

'He doesn't know me,' Fern said softly.

'If I went away. . .' The words were being forced out, one after another. 'If I went away,' Jessie faltered, 'would you marry him?'

'No!' It was a cry from the heart but instinctively Fern knew that it was true. Sure, Jessie could leave but what basis was that for a marriage between Quinn and Fern? Like murder. . .

It had the same awful feel.

'It's me who's leaving, Jessie,' Fern said savagely, tight with anger. Her words firmed as she felt how right they were. Quinn had no business putting this girl through the misery she was facing. If he was here. . . She'd like to slap his arrogant face, she thought bitterly—somehow make him realise what he was doing to his lovely young wife. What she felt for him was some sort of sick aberration. It had nothing to do with love. 'I'm leaving on Friday.'

'Leaving. . .?'

'I live in Sydney. That's where I'm going.'

'But. . .but Quinn wants you to stay.'

'And so do my aunt and uncle.' Fern lifted the now empty bottle from the little joey's mouth and spent a long time settling him back in his pouch. 'But that doesn't mean I belong on the island. My life—my career—are back in Sydney and that's where I'm going. Whatever crazy notions Quinn has about me— well, that's all they are. Crazy. . .'

'He kissed you—the night of the shark attack.'

'He did,' Fern said grimly. 'And for my pains, I let him. I was exhausted, mentally wrung out and I didn't know he was married. One kiss between strangers. Whatever Quinn likes to think about it, that's all there was to it. So. . .so you and Quinn have to decide what to do about your marriage but leave me out of the equation, Jess. No matter what you do, I don't belong here.'

I don't belong. . .

The old familiar words. They had lost none of their gall in the years since she'd first thought them.

'OK.' Jessie's voice had lost none of its sadness. 'But I would have liked...I wish, for Quinn's sake...'

She broke off and turned to face Fern, her eyes steady.

'I'd like Quinn to be happy,' she said firmly, and her eyes held Fern's with a strength Fern hadn't known the girl possessed. 'But when you say, "leave me out of it"...well, that's true for me as well. Quinn and I... Well, we have solid reasons for staying married for another few months or so. But after that, Fern... after that we'll go our separate ways and Quinn's free to do as he wishes. I just wanted you to know that. In case it makes a difference.'

How could it make a difference?

It couldn't make a difference at all.

'There are solid reasons for staying married for another few months or so...'

Fern returned to her car slowly, her mind turning over and over what she'd been told.

It didn't make sense.

Unless Jess was pregnant?

That was on the cards, too, Fern thought grimly, thinking of Jessie's exhausted look. She'd seen that look occasionally on girls who suffered badly from morning sickness.

What a mess!

Well, whatever the mess, she wanted out.

She steered the car out of the hospital car park and slowed.

There was a man...

Fern frowned.

Surely she was imagining things. She slowed as she passed an area of deep bush two hundred yards from the hospital entrance. The figure she had seen had disappeared.

You're crazy...

No.

Her internal conversation lasted the whole of five seconds. Swearing, she hauled the car to a halt, did a U-turn and headed back to the little township half a mile on the other side of the hospital.

Straight to the police.

Fern had known the police sergeant since she was a teenager. Sergeant Russell was big and gentle and deceivingly placid. Many a crook had misjudged that easy smile as the look of a man who wasn't prepared to make an effort.

There was no man who could move faster in an emergency.

He listened to Fern's story and doodled little scrawls on a pad beside him.

'You say whoever it was had a gun,' he said at last, sinking back into his chair. 'What sort of gun, do you know?'

'I don't.' Fern shook her head. 'Something long... Look, I might be mistaken. It just made me uneasy, that's all. I didn't recognise him. If he's a stranger to the island and he's shooting in the reserves...'

'If he's shooting that close to the hospital we risk pellets going through the hospital windows,' the sergeant said thoughtfully. He sighed and pulled his cap from the top of the filing cabinet. 'Guess I'd better get on with it.'

'Thanks, Sergeant...'

He smiled and held the door for her. 'My pleasure, Fern. It's good to have you back again—if only for a week or so. Oh, and Fern...'

'Yes?'

The big policeman paused, his eyes troubled.

'I was sorry about you and Sam. But...' He hesitated and then took courage into both hands. Courage was not something Sergeant Russell lacked. 'Fern, there are whispers going round the island about you and Doc Gallagher. There's nothing in it, is there, girl?'

Fern sighed. 'No, Sergeant,' she sighed. 'There's nothing in it.'

He nodded, his placid eyes watching her face. Fern wondered just how much of what she was thinking could be read there.

'He's married,' the Sergeant said heavily and Fern knew he'd read heaps.

'I know that.'

'You going back to the mainland soon?'

'On Friday.'

He nodded again. 'Just as well, Fern,' he said grimly. 'You're best well out of that lot—believe me.'

What had he meant by that?

Fern drummed her fingers on the steering wheel as she finally drove back to her uncle's. The thoughts stayed with her for the rest of the day.

'You're best off out of that lot...'

It had been a definite warning. Fern knew Sergeant Russell well enough to understand that.

Why?

There were things going on she didn't understand. Undercurrents...

Why was the policeman involved?

The shadows under Jessie's eyes drifted through and through her mind. They'd been there since the time Fern had first met her.

Jess hadn't come to Fern's wedding. Surely she'd been invited with her husband?

Why hadn't she come?

There was an insistent little voice starting up in the back of Fern's head and she didn't like it one bit.

During her training, Fern had visited a women's refuge—one where women sought sanctuary from violent men.

The shadows on their faces matched Jessie's.

No. It didn't fit. Every nerve in her body screamed out that it didn't fit—yet what else made sense?

Nothing made sense. Nothing made sense at all.

That night Fern swam until her body ached with exhaustion—and still she swam.

Her dolphins swam with her but their leaping had ceased. They swam silently by her as if sensing that she was in no mood to play.

They sensed that they couldn't help.

Fern hardly saw them. The magic of the night was wasted on her.

She swam as if escaping from a thousand demons and they never relented.

When she finally dragged herself from the water they were still with her.

So was the man with the gun.

As Fern towelled herself dry she glanced up to where sand met the grass verge and the low shrubs started pushing up from the sandy soil.

It was too dark to see him properly but she was sure that it was the same figure—a lean, tall figure with a gun, pointing to the sky.

She rang the sergeant when she got home, her uneasiness increasing.

'I haven't a clue who he is,' the policeman said, worrying with her. 'I checked the bush by the hospital after you reported it and found nothing. No signs of shooting. No spent cartridges. Nothing. A heap of tourists landed last Monday—about two hundred of them—and he must be one of the group; but there've been no reports of shooting or damage and without that I can hardly get warrants to search every one of them for a gun. Maybe he just carries a gun because it makes him feel macho.'

He hung up and Fern knew that the policeman believed what he'd said no more than Fern had.

She had him worried, too.

She didn't see Quinn until Thursday night.

Fern packed for her aunt and herself in dreary silence. The joy had bubbled out of her world.

Quinn was leaving her alone and in one sense she was grateful.

She should be grateful.

She wasn't.

She was as lost as she had ever been—as lost as she'd been in those awful weeks after her parents died.

There was nothing to look forward to.

She fell into bed late on Thursday night, knowing that she wouldn't sleep. At midday tomorrow she and her aunt would leave.

Would leave...

The words rang over and over in her head like a death knell, and it took five or six rings of the phone before the new sound finally pierced the rhythm of her inner dirge.

Finally it did, though.

Fern glanced at her watch. It was close to midnight. Her uncle wasn't home. As miserable as Fern at the thought of his wife's operation and the thought that he couldn't leave the farm untended to accompany her, he'd told Fern at eleven that he was going for a walk.

'A long walk,' he'd warned her. 'I might get full round the island before I'm tired enough to sleep tonight.'

The phone... The phone, therefore, had to be answered and there was only Fern to do it.

Fern padded down the hall and lifted the receiver.

'Fern?'

Quinn.

'Y-yes.'

'Fern, I need you.'

Ha! Fern nearly put the receiver straight back onto the cradle—but, of course, she didn't. Of course...

'Fern, I have Pete Harny here. Can you come?'

Pete. The ten year old haemophiliac.

Fern closed her eyes, envisaging trouble. 'What's wrong?'

'He's been shot.'

Not this sort of trouble. Fern's eyes opened with a start. 'I beg your pardon?'

'His parents brought him in an hour ago,' Quinn said grimly. 'I'm still not sure what happened but he has shotgun pellets in his calf and I'll have to put him to sleep to clear them. With his likelihood of internal bleeding, the sooner I get them clear the better. I've given him factor eight and pre-med and pain relief to make him dozy so if you come straight in we can do him immediately.

'Jessie will gas if she must but she won't do it if there's someone more qualified on the island. So. . .'

So.

Quinn's voice sounded strained almost to breaking point. Fern frowned. If Quinn had factor eight on the island—the mixture kept on hand whenever haemophilia was a problem—then there should be no worries with a simple surgical procedure.

So why was he so stressed?

'How bad is it?' she asked.

'Just come.' It was an order, hard and forceful.

'I'll be there in five minutes.'

She had no choice. Pete was a great kid.

There was no enthusiasm at all in Fern's voice. Sure, she'd do this for Quinn—or do it for Pete and his parents. But that would be the end.

Fern met Sergeant Russell in the hospital car park. The police sergeant was striding down the hospital steps towards the police car as Fern pulled up. His face was grim and angry.

'What on earth happened?' Fern asked and the policeman shrugged.

'I'm betting it's your character with a gun,' he told Fern savagely. 'And shooting Pete, of all kids. . .'

'But. . .but why?'

'God knows.' The policeman shrugged broad shoulders. 'Seems Pete thought he heard shots down near your cove, Fern. He loves those dolphins nearly as much as you do—and he took off out of his bedroom window to investigate without telling his parents.

'He reckoned he saw a man aiming out to sea—and he could see the dolphins. Pete yelled out and the man turned and fired. Hit him in the leg. He only just made it back home before collapsing through blood loss.'

'But... Who'd want to shoot Pete...or shoot the dolphins?'

'That's what I want to know,' the policeman said grimly. 'I'm going down to the cove now. Good luck with Pete. Poor little blighter.'

It was a nasty piece of surgery.

Pete's leg was a mass of shotgun pellets and each had to be carefully removed. Quinn worked swiftly and surely, tension etched deep on his face.

He hardly spoke to Fern—or to the nurses. Except for words of encouragement to the small boy as Fern's anaesthetic took hold, he hardly spoke at all.

He seemed... He seemed angry. Angry to the point of explosion.

Why?

Was it the senselessness of what had happened? Six months ago, before Quinn came to the island, the chance of saving Pete's life with a wound like this would have been minimal. As a haemophiliac Pete would simply have bled to death. Quinn was prepared now, though—obviously keeping stores of factor eight at hand for just such emergencies.

They worked on. Despite the undercurrents in the small theatre they worked with precision and skill.

Fern's misery was put aside as she concentrated.

Most of her thoughts were of the job in hand—but Pete wasn't so ill that other niggles couldn't intrude.

Quinn had been gentleness itself with the injured Pete. Despite his tension, he'd managed to reassure the frightened child to the point where it was easy to anaesthetise him.

How could a man with so much gentleness in his soul treat Jessie the way he did?

Did he have a child of his own on the way? Was Jessie pregnant?

Was that why the marriage had to stay together?

Quinn glanced up and found Fern's eyes on him and his eyes snapped in anger.

'Blood pressure, Dr Rycroft?' he growled, and Fern knew that he didn't need to know.

He was under more pressure than Fern. There was something going on here that she didn't understand in the least.

Finally, the last pellet lay in the kidney bowl, waiting, no doubt, to be taken proudly to school for show and tell. Quinn dressed the wound with care and grunted with satisfaction.

'I reckon we have clotting already,' he said. 'Reverse, please, Dr Rycroft.'

Five minutes later Fern removed the endotracheal tube and watched Pete's breathing revert to normal.

'There's no need for you to wait, Dr Gallagher,' she said shortly. 'I'll finish.'

'I want to talk to you.'

Geraldine was watching in the background. Fern fairly gritted her teeth.

'I don't want to talk to you.'

Quinn shrugged. He didn't move. As the little boy's eyelids fluttered open and his breathing stabilised, Quinn motioned to the nurse.

'Take him out to his mum now, Sister. He'll be frightened when he wakes. . .'

'Not Pete,' Fern said solidly. She gripped Pete's hand and held hard. 'Awake, Pete? It's over. We dug shotgun pellets out of your leg but you're fine now.'

Pete's eyes focused.

'H-how many?' he whispered and Fern raised her eyebrows in query at Quinn.

'Eight.' Quinn smiled, and it was the first smile that Fern had seen that night.

'D-don't throw them away,' Pete ordered. Then he grabbed Fern's hand. 'Fern, the dolphins...'

'Sergeant Russell's gone to check now,' Fern assured him, 'but I wouldn't mind betting they've had more sense than to get shot as well.'

'Stupid, mindless idiot,' Pete whispered, as his eyes closed again. 'Stupid, mindless idiot...'

He drifted back into sleep and Quinn motioned to Geraldine to wheel him out.

'I'm going, too,' Fern said abruptly as the stretcher disappeared towards waiting parents. She hauled off her gloves, mask and gown. 'Unless you need me for anything else, Dr Gallagher?'

'I'll always need you,' Quinn said bleakly. 'You know that, Fern.'

'I don't know anything of the kind,' Fern whispered. She closed her eyes, pain washing through her in waves. Somehow she had to find the courage to walk out of this room—walk out of Quinn Gallagher's life for ever.

She took a step forward and then another.

Quinn didn't try to stop her.

His face was as bleak as winter.

CHAPTER TEN

FERN didn't sleep.

This was her last night on the island.

What was she leaving?

Towards dawn she rose, pulled jeans and a blouse on over her swimming costume and made her way down to her cove.

There were traces of blood on the path where Pete had run the night before.

Stupid twit, she thought savagely. What sort of mindless idiot would shoot at dolphins and then turn the gun on a child when he was discovered?

If he was that stupid, surely Sergeant Russell would catch him. Whoever was responsible needed to be locked up fast.

She shed her jeans and walked steadily into the water, welcoming the cool surf on her tense body, and then swam strongly out to deep water. This would be her last swim. . .

Two hundred yards out she floated over on her back and looked back at the island.

Her home. . .

It wasn't her home. She didn't have a home. She'd never had one and she never would.

Quinn Gallagher was her home.

The errant thought crept into her mind, unbidden, and she blinked back tears. He said he loved her and the tone in his voice made her believe him. She'd never had love like that. Never.

'I'll always need you,' he'd said.

But he needed Jess and he was married to Jess.

He was married to Fern's friend, a girl who Fern couldn't hurt if her life depended on it.

Maybe... maybe, in years to come, if he and Jess were divorced...

Oh, yes. After the baby—or whatever was holding them together...

Fat chance.

She closed her eyes again, drifting lazily in the currents, and only opened them when a black form nudged her side.

A dolphin...

'Hi.' Fern managed a smile. 'Where's your mate?' She searched the water for the dolphin she had seen time and time again. The two normally swam as a pair.

She'd never seen just one.

'I hope that clod last night didn't do any damage,' she whispered and then she drew in her breath.

Her searching eyes had caught something black. Something lying on the shore at the far end of the cove where the headland started to rise from the beach.

Maybe it was only a lump of seaweed.

Maybe not.

The lone dolphin nudged Fern again and then again, as if imparting an urgent message.

They weren't stupid, these creatures.

Not as stupid as the cretin who'd been firing at them last night.

'OK,' she whispered to the dolphin, and Fern turned towards the beach. She put her head down and swam and the solitary dolphin followed her almost to shore.

It *was* the dolphin.

Of course it was the dolphin. As Fern neared the beach the mound on the sand focused into gleaming black. By the time she was wading through the shallows she could see its movement.

It was alive but stranded, thrashing uselessly on the dry sand.

'Oh, no...'

Fern ran swiftly up the beach and squatted on the

sand beside the stranded creature. Out to sea, its companion swam round in tight, anxious circles.

How on earth had it been beached?

The gun...

Of course it was the gun. A deep laceration ran through the flesh of the dolphin's back, marring the gleaming body.

It had been shot. In pain and confusion it must have tried to escape the stinging hurt and ended up beached.

Fern bit her lip. She looked down at the laceration again. It was deep—but not too deep. If she could get the dolphin down to the water again...

She couldn't. The dolphin must weigh as much as she did and it was a hundred times more slippery.

The creatures didn't come with handholds.

So...

'So, let's get you wet,' she muttered savagely, anger at this wanton act of cruelty welling through her. The dolphin's skin was drying and if he was dry for long then he'd die. The sun was already warm.

Swiftly she ran to the other end of the beach where her jeans and blouse lay abandoned. She took them quickly into the water, soaked them and then carried them up to the dolphin.

Taking care to avoid the dolphin's breathing hole, the small crescent-shaped hollow on his back, she wrung the sodden clothes out over him and then raced to the water again.

Five, six times she went until the dolphin was wet all over, its eyes watching her with weary vigilance.

'OK, sweetheart,' Fern whispered, laying the soaking clothes over him. Hopefully the wet cloth would keep most of him moist and the sun from burning his skin. 'I'm going for help.'

It took five long moments for Fern to reach the farmhouse. Her uncle was still sleeping but it wasn't her uncle Fern wanted.

She wanted a vet.

She rang the hospital and Jess answered on the first ring.

'Fern?' Her voice sounded astonished. 'What's wrong?'

Swiftly Fern outlined the problem.

'OK.' Like Quinn, Jess could also be clinically efficient. 'If it's only a flesh wound then there shouldn't be a problem—as long as we get him back in the water. I'll bring some antibiotic and someone to help lift. See you soon.'

'I'm sorry to wake you...' Fern apologised before ringing off.

'I was up, anyway.'

Someone else had suffered a sleepless night, then. The young vet's voice was tight with strain.

Fern replaced the receiver with a heavy heart. Had Fern already hurt Jessie by her presence?

There was nothing she could do about that now.

There was nothing to do but wait.

Jess arrived ten minutes later and, as promised, Jess wasn't alone.

She'd brought the heavy artillery.

Sergeant Russell—and Quinn.

'Jess thought I should see what other damage the crazy coot's done,' the policeman told Fern. Even though it was still only a little after six in the morning he was fully uniformed—and he had a service pistol at his shoulder. He grimaced down at the dolphin.

'I checked the beach last night,' he said apologetically to Jess. 'There was nothing here. I'm sure I would have found this beauty if he was here.'

'If he was injured he might have been disorientated for a while.' Jess was already kneeling in the sand, carefully inspecting the cut. 'It doesn't look as though he's been beached for too long, Fern. See his eyes? They're still quite bright and focusing. If he'd been here all night his eyes would be dull by now.'

'So, what do we do?' Fern had brought buckets from

the farmhouse and she was carefully ladling water over the dolphin's black body. She was just as carefully avoiding Quinn's eyes.

Quinn was hardly looking at Jess or the dolphin—or Fern. His eyes raked the headland as though searching for someone.

The policeman knew who.

'He's hardly likely to be out at this hour,' the sergeant said heavily, and Quinn nodded.

'OK.' Quinn turned his attention back to Jess. 'What do you want us to do?'

'Why did you come?' Fern demanded shortly. 'What if there's an emergency at the hospital?'

Quinn laid his mobile phone down on a towel beside the dolphin.

'Then I run,' he said grimly. 'But I'm staying here until this is sorted out.' His eyes were heavy and as stressed as any of them. Now he turned from Fern to Jess. 'What do you want of us, Jess?' he repeated.

'There's a tarpaulin in my truck,' Jess told him. 'The wound seems to be clean enough. The shot must have just grazed him. I can't see any evidence of lodged pellets.'

'So?' Quinn's voice was sharp and his eyes were wandering again to the headland.

'So I'll give him a shot to prevent possible infection and we get him back in the water fast.'

There was still the strange tension in Jess. Her voice was so tight it was as though she was stretched to breaking point.

'OK...'

They moved swiftly as a team. All seemed to have their private thoughts but all seemed to be keeping them to themselves as they worked.

The policeman and Quinn kept glancing up at the headland—as though they were expecting trouble any minute. Bad trouble.

It was enough to make Fern nervous herself—if she hadn't been so desperately unhappy.

Jess didn't look up. All her attention was on the dolphin, her small fingers skilfully clearing the air-hole and cleaning the wound. She filled her syringe and administered antibiotic and then, finally, she tugged the tarpaulin in and wedged it hard under the dolphin.

Then all four of them burrowed with their hands, pulling the heavy canvas under so that the dolphin was no longer lying on the sand.

He was cradled on canvas.

After that it was just a case of brute strength. It took the full strength of the four of them to drag the dolphin's dead weight back down into the shallows.

'Don't let him sink,' Jess warned as the water took most of the weight. Fern was the only one in a bathing costume but it didn't seem to matter. The other three ignored their clothing and kept wading out, supporting the dolphin's weight as he wallowed in the shallows.

They took him out to breast-deep and, under Jessie's direction, headed his nose out to sea.

Still they held on.

The dolphin hardly moved.

'It'll take time for him to regain his balance,' Jess told them. 'I want you to rock him from side, gently at first. And keep his air-hole clear.'

They worked in silence. Half an hour. More. The dolphin lay passive in their hands.

The tension in the group was almost a physical thing. As a group they were worried about the dolphin but there was more than that.

The men kept glancing up at the headland. They were waiting for something.

Someone...

Fern couldn't care. She was so aware of Quinn by her side that she wanted to weep. His sea-soaked body was touching hers, their shoulders brushing as they stood side by side in the water and their hands linked under the surface. The feel of him was almost unbearable.

She wanted to run—but she couldn't...

And then the dolphin stirred in their grasp. They felt the taut muscles rippling as his body came alive.

He seemed to flex and flex again.

'OK,' breathed Jessie. 'Let him try. Move back.'

With one accord they stepped back, their eyes all on the dolphin.

The dolphin sank slightly and a convulsive shudder ran through his gleaming black body.

It was like a dog, shaking himself after a bath.

Out to sea his mate watched and waited.

And waited.

And then the shuddering ceased. The dolphin steadied, firmed and his eyes seemed to focus. To look out to sea...

The massive muscles rippled.

He was ready.

Instinctively they stepped back further, granting him room. Granting him freedom...

And then the dolphin was moving, his gleaming body slicing through the water like a black arrow, leaping and coursing out through the shallows—to where his mate was waiting.

It was a fantastic sight. The clumsy, stranded creature was clumsy no more. He was with his mate and the pair were glistening shafts of light in the morning sun, headed for the freedom of the open sea.

They were safe.

It was all that mattered. It had to be all that mattered.

Fern was sobbing with mingled tension and relief. She stood shoulder-deep in the waves and watched them go and she had never seen anything more beautiful.

And then Quinn's arm came round her. Like Fern, he was moved almost to tears. His arm held her tight, tighter, and she was lifted off her feet against his body in the water.

The hold tightened.

He was hers, the arm said.

A wave washed hard against her, knocking her off balance, and Quinn's arms steadied her. Steadied. . .

Claiming his own!

Her face lifted to his—driven by forces stronger than either Fern or Quinn.

Forces not to be reckoned with.

And then Quinn was kissing her as though there were no one else in sight. As though there were no Jessie. . .

As though there were no tomorrow. . .

But, of course, there was.

'Quinn!'

The kiss ended as abruptly as it had begun.

The policeman's yell of warning spun Quinn round like a pistol shot. Sergeant Russell was staring up at the headland and his hand was hauling out his service revolver.

Fern was released as though she burned. She fell backwards into the waves.

There was a man on the headland and he was pointing a gun.

He was pointing a gun straight at the group in the water.

Fern floundered backwards, losing her footing almost completely but still staring up at the headland in mesmerised horror.

And Quinn had deserted her.

Quinn Gallagher was launching himself at Jess as though possessed.

'Jess. . .' he yelled desperately, and his voice held all that Fern would ever need to know. 'Jess. . .'

He reached the vet and grabbed her, twisting her body round so that he protected her, cradling her against hurt.

And then the morning was shattered into a million pieces.

A searing, red-hot pain cut across Fern's head. She

lifted her hand—and her fingers came away warm and red with blood.

It was the last thing she knew.

CHAPTER ELEVEN

FERN woke to despair.

She opened her eyes to find herself in a room she knew well. Jessie's room.

She'd slept here before.

It was different from last time she'd been here. Now there was a hospital bed where the low bed-settee had been before.

Someone had wheeled a hospital bed in here—and Fern was in it.

She didn't want to be in Jessie's room. She didn't want to be anywhere at all.

Her head hurt.

It hurt like crazy, actually, aching with a steady, pulsing throb. She put a hand up to her hair and felt bandages.

What had happened?

She didn't care.

Quinn had gone to Jess. There had been danger and Quinn had gone to Jess. Of course. Jess was his wife. No matter what he told Fern, when there was danger he'd turned to his wife.

The rest—whatever he professed he felt for Fern— was nonsense.

Fern moved her eyes a little and the movement brought the room into focus.

There was someone sitting by the bed.

Jess...

'Hey, Fern.' Jess smiled gently and Fern could see relief wash over her face. 'Welcome back.'

She didn't want to be back.

'What...what happened?' she whispered.

'You were shot,' Jess told her. 'Do you remember?'

Only too well. It made her feel ill.

'You do remember?' Jess asked anxiously. 'Quinn thought you'd just been concussed.'

'I remember. The man on the headland...' Fern winced. 'Was anyone else...was anyone else hurt?'

'The man doing the shooting was,' Jess told her. 'The sergeant had his gun—do you remember? Sergeant Russell hit him in the shoulder and he's under police guard in the next room right now. Not that he needs to be. Quinn's bandages look just like a strait-jacket.'

'But...' Fern swallowed. 'I don't understand.'

'No.' Jess smiled, and her smile was one that Fern had never seen before. She seemed young and happy and...and somehow free. As though a huge burden had been lifted from her. 'I guess you don't. But there's someone who's aching to explain the whole thing himself. He's next door now, checking your attacker, and I bet he's not being very gentle with the Elastoplast. I'll call him...'

'Quinn... No!'

It was a cry from the heart and it stopped Jess dead. Jess had risen and taken two steps toward the door. Now she turned.

'Why not, Fern?' she said gently.

'Because... Because... Jess, you know why not.'

'No, I don't,' Jess told her. 'Quinn has some explaining to do, Fern Rycroft—but he'll murder me if I do it for him.'

'Not murder...'

It was a deep, gravelly voice from the door and it made Jess jump. The young vet swivelled to find Quinn watching.

'Quinn...'

There was no mistaking the affection in her voice.

'I'll not murder you, Jess,' Quinn said severely. 'There's been enough of that lately.' He walked over to the bed and looked down at Fern. His eyes were lit by love and laughter—and, incredibly, it was all directed at Fern.

This man had dumped her...

'You're awake, my love,' he said gently and bent to kiss her. 'Thank God.' The relief came straight from the heart.

'N-no.' Fern twisted her face on her pillows, trying to turn away from the kiss. There were tears coursing down her cheeks and she could do nothing to stop them.

'Yes,' Quinn told her. He held her face still in his hands and settled a kiss on her lips. He kissed away her tears—and then released her and held out his hand to Jess.

To his wife.

'Fern, it's time we told you who this is.'

'Who. . .?' Pain and weakness were making Fern feel giddy. Quinn saw it on her face and swore.

'It's not the time for this, sweetheart,' he told her. 'You're weak as a kitten. But you need to know. Fern, this is not my wife. This is Jessica Harvey. Jess is my cousin.

'Eight months ago she started dating someone who—well, for want of a better description—turned out to be a thief and a murderer. He's also a high-ranking lawyer. She went out to dinner with him twice and on the third occasion he invited her back to his flat for a meal. He was charming and she saw no reason not to go.

'As she arrived, so did someone else—and Jess saw the man she'd gone out with murder the new arrival in cold blood.'

'But. . .but why?' The pain in Fern's head was receding. Only the dizziness stayed.

'Drugs,' Quinn said briefly. 'John Talbot was in them up to his ears. Anyway, Jess saw him fire and John Talbot saw that Jessie had witnessed the whole thing. He beat her up, badly, and threatened her with murder if she went to the police.'

'So I went to Quinn,' whispered Jess. 'Because he was like my brother. He was my friend. And Quinn went to the police.'

'But before the police reached him, Talbot disappeared,' Quinn said grimly. 'I'd promised Jess she'd be safe if she let me go to the police—but that night someone fired at Jess through her bedroom window.'

'Because she'd seen...'

'She's the only one who can convict Talbot,' Quinn said heavily. 'And he's ruthless. So...so Jess had to hide and she had to hide well. The police arranged papers so that Jess could work under my name. The charade had to continue until Talbot was caught.

'When you reported the gunman to the police, Sergeant Russell guessed who he was, though heaven knows how Talbot found Jess. We've been watching Jess like a hawk since you sighted him and I guess Talbot shot the dolphin in sheer frustration. We tried to stop Jess from going to the beach—but a wounded animal is like a homing device for her. She can no sooner refuse help than she can stop breathing. So all we could do was go with her.

'And maybe...maybe it was for the best. At least now it's finally over.'

It's finally over...

The lightening of the tension was unbelievable. Jess and Quinn stood smiling down at her with hands linked and Fern blinked and blinked again.

'You're not...You're not...'

'Quinn is my very best friend,' Jess said simply. 'But he's not my husband.' She bent to kiss Fern on the cheek.

'And he is not my love, nor will he ever be. When Quinn saw Talbot on the cliff he assumed Talbot was aiming at me. I guess he was—but he was too far away to see properly. So while Quinn was doing his cousinly best to save me, the love of his life was getting herself close to murdered.' She twinkled up at Quinn.

'And my dear, calm, sensible Quinn nearly went crazy.'

'Jessie...' Quinn's voice was a warning.

Quinn was smiling at his cousin but his eyes were giving her an urgent message.

Jess laughed.

'I know,' she twinkled. 'I can see when I'm not wanted. I'll just get back to the loves of *my* life then, shall I? Two wallabies, one parrot and one echidna.'

And she walked out, laughing.

Fern and Quinn were left facing each other.

There was a long silence. All of a sudden Fern felt absurdly shy.

And as if nightingales were starting to sing, somewhere in the region of her heart.

'Can you forgive me, Fern?' Quinn asked softly. He sat down on the bed and gathered her two hands to his chest. 'If you knew how I wanted to tell you. . . But it was crazy. If I broke. . . If I broke and told you, then I couldn't keep appearances up with Jess—and Jessie's life was forfeit. And I'd persuaded her to go to the police in the first place.'

'I. . . There's nothing to forgive,' Fern whispered.

The nightingales were singing louder and louder. The dizziness was there in force, washing over her in lovely, misty waves that were all about drowning.

Drowning in Quinn's dark eyes.

'Then you'll marry me, my heart?'

'I don't. . .' Fern shook her head. This was crazy. 'Quinn, I can't. . .'

'Can't marry me?' Incredibly, his eyes were anxious.

'Can't decide.' Fern dredged up dignity with a superhuman effort. 'I'm not supposed to get married.'

'Yes, you are. You were getting married the first time I saw you, if you remember. You were just getting married to the wrong man.'

'But not. . .'

'Not to the man you loved.' Quinn took her in his arms with a tenderness that took her breath away. 'No, my darling. Not to the man you loved. Or the man who loved you. The man who loves you is right here, Fern, my darling girl, my crazy, crazy doctor bride.

'And I know I shouldn't pressure you when you're still suffering from concussion but if I don't then I'm afraid I'll go away and you'll think up all those sensible reasons why you shouldn't marry someone who loves you more than life itself. So. . .'

'So?' Fern whispered.

He put her away from him and held her at arm's length.

'So if you want to put your head on the pillows then you have to do what the doctor orders.'

Fern's lips curved into the beginnings of a smile.

'And the prescription?'

'One husband,' he said solemnly. 'Slightly used. I've had a practice run, you might say, but then so have you. You were a practice bride. Now it's your turn to be a real one. . .'

'Oh, Quinn. . .' She didn't know whether to laugh or cry.

'That's not what you're supposed to say,' he told her severely.

'What. . .what am I supposed to say?'

He smiled then, his lovely, laughing smile that was a caress all by itself.

'Just say "I will", my lovely Fern,' he said gently. 'Nothing else matters.'

Nothing else matters.

And suddenly it didn't.

Fern looked up at the man she loved and she found the answer to all her questions in his eyes.

She was loved.

She was home.

'I will,' she whispered, but Quinn hardly heard.

Fern's eyes had said it all.

CHAPTER TWELVE

IT WAS four long weeks before the wedding could take place legally and then they were forced to wait another interminable two. Those six weeks were spent by Fern in Sydney, supervising her aunt's convalescence.

Fern had promised to wed on the island but to wed without her aunt's presence was unthinkable. Even Quinn wouldn't think of it.

The wait did give Fern time to collect her thoughts. Or almost.

Quinn telephoned twice a day and each time he rang Fern's thoughts were scattered like dandelion seeds in a high wind.

Still—there was time for other things.

There was time for Bill Fennelly's tuberculosis tests to come back positive—and for him to begin to respond to treatment. He was well enough to accept a wedding invitation.

There was time for Fern to see Sam and Lizzy and wish them well and for Sam to do the same for her. Sam and Lizzy were planning an island wedding of their own.

There was time to see Aunt Maud well on the mend and time besides. . .

Too much time.

Six interminable weeks. . .

On their wedding day the chapel was deserted.

The whole island was present to see Fern Rycroft married but bride and groom had chosen another venue. The vicar, bemused but acquiescent, carried his altar to Fern's cove.

There was no satin.

Fern married in a white gown of fine cotton, simply

cut, with a low neckline, bare sleeves and a soft, flowing skirt that fluttered lightly round her legs in the breeze.

She left her red-gold head bare and her feet were bare too.

She was an island bride.

'A lovely bride,' the islanders had said of that first bride, the Fern of several weeks ago.

Now there was hardly a dry eye on the beach but they weren't saying 'a lovely bride'.

'Our lovely Fern,' they whispered as they watched her make her vows. 'Our Fern...'

'Our Fern,' her aunt and uncle murmured with love and pride, but Quinn had a different adjective for his lovely bride.

'You may now kiss the bride,' the vicar said at last, eyeing this handsome couple with placid ease. If ever a marriage would work, he thought contentedly, this one would.

Man and wife...

'My Fern.' Quinn's words sounded out as a vow as he gathered his island bride close and Fern lifted her lips to receive his kiss.

To receive all his love with all her heart.

'My Quinn.'

Their marriage vows were sealed for ever.

And were blessed...

The waves rolled in. They'd roll in for ever, Fern thought gladly. On us, on our children and on our children's children.

And out to sea a pair of dolphins leapt high in the rolling smell of glistening ocean.

The world was theirs.

And who was to say their thoughts weren't exactly the same?

Look next month for Jess's own wonderful story in
PRESCRIPTION—ONE BRIDE

MILLS & BOON

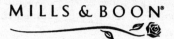

Books for enjoyment this month...

CRISIS FOR CASSANDRA	Abigail Gordon
PRESCRIPTION—ONE HUSBAND	Marion Lennox
WORTH WAITING FOR	Josie Metcalfe
DR RYDER AND SON	Gill Sanderson

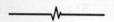

Treats in store!

Watch next month for these absorbing stories...

TRUSTING DR SCOTT	Mary Hawkins
PRESCRIPTION—ONE BRIDE	Marion Lennox
TAKING RISKS	Sharon Kendrick
PERFECT PRESCRIPTION	Carol Wood

Available from:
W.H. Smith, John Menzies, Volume One, Forbuoys, Martins,
Woolworths, Tesco, Asda, Safeway and other paperback stockists.

Readers in South Africa - write to:
IBS, Private Bag X3010, Randburg 2125.

MILLS & BOON

Back by Popular Demand

BETTY NEELS

COLLECTOR'S EDITION

A collector's edition of favourite titles from one of the world's best-loved romance authors.

Mills & Boon are proud to bring back these sought after titles, now reissued in beautifully matching volumes and presented as one cherished collection.

Don't miss these unforgettable titles, coming next month:

Title #9   WISH WITH THE CANDLES
Title #10 BRITANNIA ALL AT SEA

Available wherever
Mills & Boon books are sold

Available from WH Smith, John Menzies, Forbuoys, Martins, Tesco, Asda, Safeway and other paperback stockists.

One to Another

A year's supply of Mills & Boon® novels— absolutely FREE!

Would you like to win a year's supply of heartwarming and passionate romances? Well, you can and they're FREE! Simply complete the missing word competition below and send it to us by 28th February 1997. The first 5 correct entries picked after the closing date will win a year's supply of Mills & Boon romance novels (six books every month—worth over £150). What could be easier?

PAPER	B A C K	WARDS
ARM		MAN
PAIN		ON
SHOE		TOP
FIRE		MAT
WAIST		HANGER
BED		BOX
BACK		AGE
RAIN		FALL
CHOPPING		ROOM

Please turn over for details of how to enter ☞

How to enter...

There are ten missing words in our grid overleaf. Each of the missing words must connect up with the words on either side to make a new word—e.g. PAPER-BACK-WARDS. As you find each one, write it in the space provided, we've done the first one for you!

When you have found all the words, don't forget to fill in your name and address in the space provided below and pop this page into an envelope (you don't even need a stamp) and post it today. Hurry—competition ends 28th February 1997.

**Mills & Boon® One to Another
FREEPOST
Croydon
Surrey
CR9 3WZ**

Are you a Reader Service Subscriber?   Yes ❑   No ❑

Ms/Mrs/Miss/Mr _____

Address _____

_____ Postcode _____

One application per household.

You may be mailed with other offers from other reputable companies as a result of this application. If you would prefer not to receive such offers, please tick box.   ❑

C496
A